GATOR'S CHALLENGE

Bitten Point #4

EVE LANGLAIS

Chapter 1

A LONG TIME AGO, a young girl loved a boy from the wrong side of the swamp. Everyone told her to stay away. *He's bad news.* He was a Mercer, the family everyone talked about with a sneer and contempt.

Good girls shouldn't associate with bad boys. She never claimed to be a good girl, and no one told her what to do. She made her own decisions, and she decided she wanted him.

From the first moment she met Wes in high school—a high school she was late attending since her mother insisted good girls went to Catholic school—she saw right away that the boy with the lanky hair and leather jacket had potential. For one thing, he turned out to be a lot different from what the rumors claimed. Wes wanted better for himself and his family. Wes had goals and dreams, dreams he shared under shaded boughs in between kisses. Back then, she believed they would have a happily ever after. Believed a boy when he said he loved her.

Young, in love, and innocent—until the day he dumped her. For her own good, so he claimed, the icing on a bitter, heartbroken cake—and she meant that quite literally. The jerk broke her heart on Valentine's Day, right after he ate the cupcake she'd made that said "I love you."

"You're better off without me," he said, wisps of smoke curling from his nostrils, as he couldn't help a nervous drag from his cigarette. A nasty habit she planned to cure him of, along with his tendency to wear black shirts with heavy metal bands on them.

"I don't understand. You're breaking up with me?" She couldn't miss the nod of his head. "Why?"

"Because."

"Because isn't an answer."

"It is when you're a Mercer."

"You promised you'd love me forever."

"I lied."

He didn't love her. He'd never loved her. All that they'd shared? A big, fat lie.

Those words smashed her heart into pieces. Such a mournful meow moment. Such an eye opener. It was also the first time she'd truly let her Latina rage overcome her.

Anger led her to cleanse herself of him by burning every single picture and thing he'd given her—even that stupidly adorable stuffed gator wearing the shades. For days, weeks, even years afterward, she claimed to hate him—stupid, rotten jerk. She believed that with all of her being. Yet, her heart still pitter-pattered every time she caught a glimpse or heard Wes's voice. It irked her to no end that she never felt the same kind of pitter-patter for her husband. Poor Andrew, he just didn't inspire that kind of passion.

And she missed the spurt of excitement, that quick rush of her heart and the heat of anticipation. So many times, Melanie couldn't help but long for what could have been.

We could have been so great together if he'd given us a chance.

She forgot all her foolish dreams when she shot him. She should probably add she'd shot her husband, too.

Rewind a few moments, though, to the hour before she pulled the trigger. Picture her as she alternated sitting on the couch and pacing her living room floor, a polished oak that required a little too much wood polish to stay pretty. Imagine her chewing her fingers after promising Daryl, her brother, that she wouldn't do anything foolish. As if anybody who knew her would believe that.

At the click of a key in the lock, Melanie stood from the couch, every atom in her body trembling. Ever since she'd gotten the call about the explosion at Bittech, she'd wondered, *Was Andrew in there when the bombs went off?*

At least they *thought* it was explosives that had taken down the medical institute. How else to explain the massive boom and rumble resulting in the utter destruction of a building made to withstand hurricanes?

Is my husband dead or alive? And if alive, had he played a part in the demolition?

Once upon a time, Melanie would have claimed no

way. Her benign husband, with his love of documentaries and a sizzling game of chess, would never stoop to something so heinous. But that was before she and her friends discovered the truth behind rumors of Bittech Institute running an underground installation that experimented on shifters. More sobering, Andrew had to know about the testing, the kidnappings, and the monsters killing innocent folk in and around town. It shocked her to realize, as more and more of the truth unfolded, that she didn't know the man she'd slept beside for years.

Have I truly been so blind?

Told you not to mate him. Her inner feline never had cared for Andrew. As if she'd trust her cat after she'd been so wrong about Wes.

The bright red door, which she'd painted to stand out from the others in the cookie-cutter neighborhood, swung open, and through it stepped Andrew.

Her husband.

Possibly a traitor to all shifter kind.

Even now, she didn't want to believe it. Believing it meant reevaluating her entire life since high school. It meant admitting she'd made a colossal mistake in marrying Andrew.

Being wrong meant listening to her brother's taunting "I told you so." Daryl never had liked her husband.

Andrew walked in as if he still held the right.

I'll be the judge of that.

The gun that she'd removed from the safe felt heavy in her hands. She still raised and steadied it in his direction. Usually, she wouldn't touch the thing. Weapons were for prey. As a panther shifter, she preferred to let her predator take care of problems menacing her. Yet, her cat couldn't ask questions, so she brought out the weapon Andrew had bought a few years ago as protection against neighborhood vandals. The reality that he could shift into a bear and tear the head off any idiot who entered never factored into the equation of whether they should get a weapon. When it came to his wild side, Andrew was woefully lacking.

That's not the only thing he lacks, her kitty slyly reminded.

It wasn't always about size, although, in this case, Melanie had the furry balls to keep the weapon aimed with a threatened, "Don't take another step."

Despite the warning, Andrew didn't listen or even spare her a glance. He never spared her anything, not his attention or his love. He definitely never let her borrow his nice and shiny BMW. She got stuck with the practical mini van. She enjoyed her petty revenge by sending the boys with their daddy in his pretty car—with slushies.

Tossing his keys on the side table, Andrew dropped his briefcase. He still had yet to acknowledge her or the weapon she aimed.

"I said don't move. Or, even better, get out."

Yes, run. So we can chase. Her cat was in dire need of exercise.

Her words finally drew his attention. Andrew raised his gaze to meet hers. No surprise. No trepidation. Only disdain, an expression she'd never seen on him before. "Is that any way to greet me, dear wife?"

"It is when I've been listening to reports all night long about the stuff happening at Bittech."

"Did the town gossips run to tattle on me?" He smirked.

"It's more than gossip."

"You're right. It is." His smile taunted and threw her for a loop. How entirely out of character. Who was this man?

"You're not going to deny it."

"Why would I? It's true? Now, put that thing down." He took a step toward her.

She steadied her hands. "I said don't move."

He didn't bother to hide his amusement. "Or you'll what, Melanie? Shoot me? We both know you don't have the guts. So stop wasting my time. You need to pack a bag. Quickly. Wake the boys, too. We all need to leave."

"I'm not going anywhere with you." And neither were her boys.

"I'm sorry, did I say you had a choice?" Andrew's hand shot out and grabbed hold of the wrist of the hand holding the gun. He possessed a stronger wiry strength than she would have credited. He held her with ease.

In her mind, her cat snarled, not liking this unexpected turn of events.

"Asshole. Let go of me. You can't force me to go anywhere." She struck at him with her free hand, but the man she thought she knew, the one who couldn't stand the sight of blood, the one who wouldn't even squish a spider, held fast. Held her firmly.

When did he become so strong?

"Shut your annoying mouth. I've heard quite enough from you." With his free hand, he slapped her.

Slapped. Me!

Her head rocked to the side. She tasted blood as the edge of her teeth cut her lip. She didn't know what shocked her more, the fact Andrew had hit her or the fact she didn't shift into her cat and rip his face off. Her feline certainly growled inside her mind.

Come on out, kitty. Show him who's more vicious.

Rowr! Which, translated from kitty speak, meant with pleasure.

Except, when she pulled at her inner beast, tried to coax her out... Nothing.

I can't shift!

Fear made her eye Andrew differently, with a reminder of what the rumors claimed. "What did you do to me? My panther can't come out."

"Much as I'd love to play with your pussy," he said with a leer that just looked plain unnatural, "I know what your claws are capable of. So I gave you a little something to keep you in your skin."

"You drugged me!" She screeched, struggling anew, only to reel as he cuffed her again, a stronger blow that made her see little birdies.

Swat at one and let's see how they taste.

Blink.

"Don't hit her." The low, growled warning came from behind Andrew.

Her heart stuttered.

Usually, running into Wes meant trying to hide her discomfort—and resisting an urge to kick him in the manparts. Not this time. She'd never been happier to see the big Mercer.

Andrew's in trouble. She practically sang the words in her head. Despite her throbbing cheek, she still turned a triumphant smile on Andrew. "Yeah, Andrew. Don't hit me." *Or Wes will hit you back harder.*

Meow. Nothing like the prospect of a smackdown to make her feline regain some pride.

"You meddle in things that are none of your business, gator," Andrew barked over his shoulder as Wes filled the open doorway—and she meant filled, considering the width of his shoulders.

"Men don't hit women." A flat statement.

Chauvinistic, but she'd take it.

"And employees don't backtalk to their bosses. So mind your place, gator, or you won't have that cushy job anymore. I brought you along to help me, not give me lip."

"Help you?" Melanie managed to utter the words through frozen lips.

Peeking at Wes, she noted his stony expression as she waited for him to refute Andrew's words. Even better, she hoped Wes would slap her bastard husband upside the head. Instead, Wes tightened his lips.

He's not here to save me. The realization hurt more than it should have.

"How could you?" she whispered. *How could he betray me again?*

He said the same thing to her now that he had when they'd broken up and she'd cried why.

"Because."

But Melanie wasn't a teenage girl anymore, and as she slammed her foot down on Andrew's—*take that, you bastard*—forcing him to loose her gun-wielding hand, she retorted, "Because isn't an answer."

Neither was shooting first her husband or her ex boyfriend—*Bang! Bang!*—but it sure felt damned good.

Chapter 2

SHE SHOT ME!

Wes couldn't believe it, and yet, at the same time, he couldn't blame Melanie. How must it look, him showing up on her doorstep, Andrew claiming Wes came to help?

It looks exactly how things are. I work for her husband, and between the pair of us, we're tied for the asshole of the year award. The fact that Wes didn't obey willingly didn't factor. In Melanie's eyes, he had just become the enemy.

And she'd acted.

She shot both him and Andrew.

Another man might have lost his shit at that point. Probably retaliated, too. Andrew sure as hell wasn't happy she had the guts to fire that gun. But Wes? Fuck, he loved that brave side of her. *That Latin fire of hers always was sexy.*

What he hated was seeing the look of frustrated realization in her eyes as Andrew chuckled, the harmless blanks she'd fired leaving merely a bruise on the flesh.

"Stupid, stupid Melanie. Did you really think I'd leave a loaded gun around here, knowing you might use it on me?"

Dawning understanding shaped her visage as she glanced at the useless weapon in her hand. "You filled it with duds. You knew this day would come."

"Of course I did. And it's past time that you grasped I'm not the teddy bear you thought I was." Andrew's malicious smile did not resemble his usual dough-faced demeanor. Beneath the nerd façade lurked a bad man, a man who kept getting worse.

A bad man I have to work for.

Told you we should have eaten him. His gator never had liked the asshole—and that began before Andrew had hooked up with Melanie. But he hated him twice as much after.

"It's all true then, isn't it? You knew about the things happening in our town. The disappearances, the deaths," Melanie stated, taking a slow step back.

"I knew and helped cover them up. Amazing what a lot of money and a few choice threats can do. Did you know most people have a price?"

"What was yours?" she asked Andrew.

"No one paid me to join in. I immediately saw the potential when my father drew me into the secret a few years ago."

"You should have said no. Done the right thing."

"Who are you to say what's right?" Andrew rocked on his heels and held out his hands wide. "We are doing cutting edge things with gene manipulation. Achieving wonders you can't even begin to imagine."

"Wonders like the lizard monster who killed those people? What about Harold? That dog thing you made out of that poor B&B owner's son."

"With success comes some bumps."

"I'd say a psychotic flying lizard who craves human flesh is a little more than a bump."

And she doesn't even know the half of it, Wes thought.

"You are only focusing on the negative. You forgot about the positive."

"I don't see how any of this is positive."

"Because you lack vision. But you'll understand. Soon everyone will see what we've been doing." A zealous light gleamed in Andrew's eyes, the scariest illumination of all.

"They'll see you're a monster."

Andrew's lips tightened. "Enough of the stalling and name calling, dear wife. Gather the boys. We have to go."

Wes could predict the words before she uttered them with a triumphant smile. "The boys aren't here."

With a narrowed gaze, Andrew snapped, "What have you done with them?"

"Kept them safe from you," she spat.

"Perhaps you should have worried about keeping yourself safe. Grab her."

The order Wes dreaded had come. For a moment, he thought about telling Andrew to fucking get her himself —and then smacking him when he did.

However, there were lives at stake, lives he cared about.

We care for Melanie. A warm reminder from the cold part of him. A reminder he ignored as he lunged for her.

But she darted out of reach. She always was fleet of foot, something he counted on.

Turning on her heel, Melanie darted into the bowels of her home, leaving him with a glimpse of hair bouncing and pert ass moving.

Damn, I love that ass.

Loved. He'd lost all rights to that perky butt years ago.

"What the hell are you waiting for?" Andrew yelled. "Go after her. I need her to tell me where the boys are."

Say no. Say fucking no. He bit back the words and did as Andrew ordered. He went after Melanie, perhaps not as quickly as he was capable of, perhaps not even as efficiently. This was one hunt he didn't want to win.

As he turned the corner of the hall, he noted four doors, all shut. Opening door number one, he noted a guest bedroom, done in a soothing pale yellow. The bed bore a flowered comforter and fluffy pillows.

No Melanie.

On to door number two. A pair of matching beds, perfect for twin boys. The beds were empty, the comforters covered in grinning sharks, smooth and untouched. On the walls hung posters of *Transformers*, *Star Wars*, and even one for the *Jungle Book*.

Toys lay scattered on the floor—cars and dinosaurs and building blocks. A room for Melanie and Andrew's boys, boys that could have been Wes's if he'd not fucked up and let her go.

Speaking of letting go, he'd spent enough time in the empty room to know she'd not come this way.

Out in the hall, he inhaled. As a shifter, even in his human form, some of his senses remained enhanced. Take his sense of smell, for example. A myriad bouquet of aromas came to him, but the freshest—and most enticing—belonged to Melanie. Even though he knew she didn't hide behind the next door, he opened it, mostly because he wanted to hear that note of impatience from Andrew as he yelled, "Did you grab her?"

Peeking into the bathroom with its white subway tile, dual sink, and the shower curtain with more sharks on it, he could say with utmost honesty, "Not yet."

One door left at the end of the hall. Her scent led right to it. He paused a moment before gripping the knob and opening the door to the master bedroom. The room where Melanie slept—and had sex with that fucking a-hole Andrew.

Irrational jealousy burned inside him at the view of the king-sized bed with its red and gold comforter and the stack of fluffy pillows.

Tear it to shreds. His inner gator knew what it wanted to do. It had no problem admitting jealousy, a jealousy he no longer had a right to.

Stepping farther into the room, he noted the open window. A slight breeze fluttered the curtains covering it.

As he heard an impatient Andrew finally coming to investigate for himself, Wes moved to the window and leaned out for a peek just as his boss entered the room.

"Did you find her?"

Looking out, he spotted Melanie perched atop the

fence separating her yard from the next. His eyes met hers and locked for a moment.

I see you.

I hate you and will tear your guts out if you come near me, hers replied.

He almost grinned.

"No sign of her, boss," he said, holding her gaze. He gave her a slow wink. "Looks like she got away. Do you want me to go outside and see if I can pick up her trail?"

"No. We need to leave before her brother or one of his friends show up. She's not that important in the grand scheme of things."

Maybe not to Andrew, but in Wes's world, she still meant way too much.

And you let her get away.

Chapter 3

PERCHED ATOP THE FENCE, Melanie heard Wes lie to Andrew, and while it didn't forgive his many trespasses, she couldn't help but grudgingly thank him for it. His lie let her escape.

Maybe I'll kill him quickly instead of slowly.

As her feet hit the ground on the other side of the fence, she paused to listen.

Her ears perked as she heard Andrew tell Wes not to bother going after her. Good thing because, with the mood she was in, she might have gone looking for a sharp tool and turned Wes into a purse. Bloodthirsty?

Yes. And she felt no shame. Some people resorted to yoga when pissed. Others gorged on ice cream or hit the gym. When she felt particularly annoyed with Wes—which was every time she caught sight of him—she tended to hit Bayou Bite for deep-fried gator chunks. The un-evolved kind, of course, but that didn't stop her from wishing the juicy morsels in that yummy crunch belonged to Wes. *I'd love to bite him.*

Now if only the bite wasn't somewhere naughty below the belt as he held her hair and moaned encouragement.

Sigh.

So many years gone by and she still couldn't wipe those erotic memories from her mind.

A voice from behind almost made her squeak.

"Are you okay?"

Brother Daryl, here to keep an eye on her while she helped them with the plan.

Oh yes, they had a plan, a plan that had almost gone to hell because of a few factors they'd not imagined.

"Wes is in cahoots with Andrew."

With his lips pulled tight, Daryl uttered a low growl. "I fucking knew it. Knew there was no way he couldn't have seen anything more concrete about Bittech's involvement while he was working there."

"Yeah, well, he knows, and him showing up to act as a henchman almost screwed the plan. Andrew sent him after me."

"Fucking bastard! Good thing you were quick."

"He let me go." Even now, she still didn't get it. Why hadn't he come after her? Wes could have easily caught her, yet he'd winked and lied to Andrew. She didn't understand it, and the confusion about his actions annoyed her. "Did I stall them long enough for you to get the tracking device put onto the car?"

Daryl grinned, his white teeth gleaming in the darkness. "Fucking right I did. Now we sit back, watch, and see where they go."

Because watching was the whole purpose in leaving Melanie in her house. Given everyone now knew about the nefarious deeds Bittech was involved in, everyone wanted to know where they'd packed up and gone to. The new Bittech location needed to be found—and taken apart. The plan was to let Andrew lead them right to it.

"What are you guys gonna do when we find out where they've gone?"

That remained the question no one had an answer to. Usually, in the cases of shifters behaving badly, the Shifter High Council got involved. And, by involved, Melanie meant they usually terminated the misbehaving culprit. Keeping their secret at all costs was the prime rule they all lived by. Break that rule and pay the price.

But what happened when the ones breaking the rules did so at the behest of a corrupt SHC? What recourse was there when those elected to protect them were guilty? The knowledge that Parker, a councilman, was involved and spearheading the experiments on shifters threw them all for a loop. If they couldn't trust the SHC, then who did that leave to save them?

The dilemma plagued her as Daryl drove her back to her Aunt Cecilia's house. Since her aunt had gone west for a few weeks to visit her daughter, it was where Melanie had stashed the boys, along with her mom, to keep them out of harm's way. It still surprised her Andrew had come back to their house. When they'd hatched the plan, a part of her figured, if he was guilty, he'd just run.

He hadn't. Andrew had come looking for her and the boys. A good thing she'd sent them away ahead of time. She'd not expected things to get so crazy so quickly, nor for Andrew to have help. Even her ace in the hole, the gun, hadn't helped since it was loaded with blanks.

He knew this day would come. He'd proved more prepared than her.

It surprised her that Andrew seemed so interested in taking her and the boys with him. He'd never shown much of an interest in his progeny—achieved after several rounds of fertility at Bittech. Mixed shifter castes did not reproduce easily.

I don't care if he's their father. He's not getting his grubby paws on them. The boys would stay with her no matter what happened next with Andrew. She'd have to ask around for a good divorce lawyer.

We could save time and annoyance by simply killing him. Her feline didn't take to their mate's betrayal kindly.

The headlights on Daryl's car lit the small house at the end of the driveway. Not a big place, with weathered green siding, a front yard replete with gnomes and pink flamingoes. Aunt Cecilia loved bright colors and fanciful garden ornaments.

Through the windshield, Melanie could see the aluminum door at the front hanging drunkenly, the thicker wooden one wide open. More terrifying of all was the sight of her mother wailing on the step, a hand held to her head, blood streaking through her fingers.

The hair on Melanie's body hackled.

"Mama!" No sooner had the car skidded to a stop than both she and Daryl spilled out and ran to their mother. She couldn't help but smell the lingering trace of something reptilian. Her heart raced a mile a minute, and she couldn't stop a fluttery panic.

"What happened?" Daryl barked.

"I tried to stop it," her mother wailed. "But the monster thing batted me aside as if I were nothing. Then he licked me." A shudder went through her mother as she grimaced. "And I froze. I couldn't move a muscle as that monster took the bambinos."

"My boys? He took my boys?" Melanie's voice pitched as the horror of what happened hit.

"I am so sorry. I couldn't stop him. The lizard monster came and took them both."

It took everything Melanie had not to shriek. But she couldn't help grabbing her hair in two fists and pulling hard. She needed the pain to focus, anything to not think of what might happen to her precious babies.

Daryl knelt before their mother. "This creature, did he fly away with them? Run off? Do you know which way it went? Perhaps I can pick up its trail."

A shake of her head and their mother explained. "I don't think he did either. I heard an engine. Someone drove that thing here, and he took the bambinos." Fresh tears and wails shook her mother's body, and even though Melanie wanted to shake and curse and scream herself, instead, she wrapped the rotund body in her arms and rocked with her mothers. Tears streamed down her cheeks.

That bastard took my babies.

And she was going to get them back.

She just didn't know how. No one did.

Daryl put in a call to Caleb, who arrived soon after with Renny and Luke and his mother. Given Constantine was holed up in a motel recuperating from his rescue of Aria, they left him out of the loop.

No point in disturbing him until there was something they could do.

"Where did that monster take them?" Since Melanie had asked this question at least a dozen times, no one bothered to reply. Andrew, Wes, the lizard monster, everyone involved with Bittech had vanished without leaving a clue or trace.

The GPS tracker they'd thought would solve all their problems and lead them to Andrew, and all the other asshats involved in the Bittech madness, proved a bust. Somehow, Andrew, or Wes, had figured it out. When Daryl went speeding after it, Melanie balancing the tablet displaying a map and a blinking icon, they found the tracker less than a mile from town on the side of the road.

Seeing it there, along with Rory's teddy, brought to her lips a much-needed scream.

On her knees, she wailed to the sky. Screamed in rage. Fear. Anguish.

Yowled until her brother forced her to move.

So much for Daryl's plan. *My babies are lost.* And she didn't know how to find them.

After that failure, they'd returned to her mother's house. They talked in circles, but nothing, nothing goddammit, brought her babies back!

"I need some air," she mumbled, unable to listen to another word. They could tell her only so many times,

"Don't worry. We'll find them," before she got an urge to scream again.

As she went to slip out the front door, her brother grabbed her arm. "You shouldn't go outside alone."

"Why not?" She uttered a mournful laugh. "Maybe if I'm out there, they'll come and take me, too. At least then I'd be with Rory and Tatum."

"We'll find them, sis. I promise."

Except this was one big-brother promise Daryl couldn't keep.

Melanie stepped out of her house, leaving Daryl, Cynthia, Caleb, and Renny to keep hashing out ideas. The moist air of the bayou filled her lungs, and she could have cried.

How she'd missed the smell of home, this home, the one she grew up in. Her cookie-cutter neighborhood, while nice, didn't have a familiar feel and welcoming vibe. She hated living in the 'burbs, even if she did have a three-bedroom house with two and a half baths—a sign, according to her mother, that she'd made it.

She'd have traded her gorgeous ensuite in a heartbeat for a happy marriage.

But at least I have my boys.

Missing boys. Sob.

She sat on the step and drew her knees to her chin. Hugging them, she rocked, the ache inside her hard to bear.

I failed them as a mother. She'd miscalculated so badly. She should have sent them farther. Should have gone with them.

Instead, because she'd misjudged the depravity of her husband, they were gone. But not dead. *Oh, please no.*

Surely she'd know if they'd left this plane of life. And if they had, she might just—

The phone in her back pocket buzzed. Odd for many reasons. One, it was well past midnight. Two, pretty much anyone who would call her this late was in the house at her back.

With shaking hands, she pulled the cell from her pants pocket and, upon seeing the caller ID, answered.

"You bastard, where are the boys?"

"Watch your mouth or you won't ever see them again," Andrew threatened.

"I'm sorry." The apology left a sour taste in her mouth.

"You should be. After all, you were the one who tried to hide them first. Just not very well."

"I want to see them."

"You will, but only if you follow my instructions to a tee. Starting with tell no one I've called."

She didn't, not until she'd managed to slip far away. Then she did a quick call, but only to say, "I've gone to find the boys."

The problem with walking eyes wide open into a trap was not knowing if she'd ever escape.

Chapter 4

WE SHOULD LEAVE.

His gator expressed his displeasure and had been doing so since they left Bitten Point. Wes couldn't blame him.

I wish I could go back in time. Change things so he wouldn't find himself here, in this place. Trapped in this nightmare.

Wes paced the room they'd given him at the new and supposedly improved Bittech Institute. Although calling it an institute sounded too nice. Try more like fucking torturous dungeon, only this time it sat above ground.

The new place wasn't even all that far from the original, but this new location had a hell of a lot more security, layers upon layers, and barracks for the employees working within.

No more wandering into town and flapping loose gums. No more curious residents asking questions.

Bye-bye, freedom.

Then again, Wes had lost his freedom the day he made his choice. *Do as we say, or else.*

The "or else" had made his decision a no-brainer. Still, though, the bitter pill proved hard to swallow.

A pack of smokes came out of his shirt pocket, and he tapped one out. He snagged the filtered tip with his lips as he yanked out a lighter. He paused as he caught a glimpse of a smoke detector on the wall and the sprinklers in the ceiling.

"Fuck." Stupid anti-smoking a-holes. Couldn't light a cigarette anywhere indoors these days without getting into trouble or causing thousands in water damage as automated fire systems engaged.

Stepping out of his room—if you could call the cell-like square a room with its double bed, desk, single chair and television—he headed along the bland gray corridor to the bright red Exit sign gleaming at the end. The hall on this third floor of the employee housing was quiet this time of the morning, unlike the previous eve when the guards and doctors, brought over to the new place, moved in.

The majority of the commotion died down around midnight, but Wes never did manage to fall asleep, not with the image of Melanie, betrayal shining in her eyes, reminding him of his douche-bag status.

I betrayed her.

His gator harrumphed. *You betrayed all of our own kind.*

And the worst part? He knew what people would say. *Not surprised at all he turned out to be a traitor. He is a Mercer after all.*

The stigma of his name followed him and, in this case, proved well deserved.

Stepping out of the compound, Wes noted in the distance the guards patrolling not only the entrance—which required identity cards and thumbprint swipes—but also those guarding the perimeter, not all of them human.

It seemed Bittech Institute wasn't trying very hard to hide anymore. Wes had to wonder how long before the outside world took note.

Hopefully it would take a while before an intrepid human drove the two miles down the long, winding drive to the new institute and noted the monsters roaming around. It didn't bear thinking what would happen if the world found out monsters lived among them.

The brisk dawn air hit him, and he inhaled deeply, filling his lungs, a man grasping at a freedom taunting him just out of reach.

The fresh, crisp air and wide-open sky teased Wes. It called him. *Leave this place. Swim free. Hunt for pleasure, not for others*.

Funny how that voice sounded an awful lot like his inner beast.

The freedom he'd lost chafed. The fresh air taunted him with—

The acrid smoke curled from the tip of the cigarette he lit, wiping away the torturous reminder of what he couldn't have. He pushed back against the insidious whispers telling him to escape.

If I leave, what will happen?

It didn't bear contemplating, and he wouldn't second-guess his choices now, not when he knew he'd make the same decision again.

Regret was for pussies. A real man made his bed, and he fucking slept in it, even if it was lined in nails, rusty ones.

Argh. He threw the cigarette, but its feathery weight worked against him. The lit butt caught in a gust of wind and flew back toward him.

Fucking hell. The discarded smoke hit the one rip in his jean-clad thigh and singed. He flicked it away, but the damage was done. A hint of red there and a dose of heat to sear the skin—*mmm, barbecue.*

Not funny, you sick bastard.

As Wes rebuked his inner gator, he slapped himself, only to hear a voice he never thought to hear again after last night.

"You're slapping the wrong part of your body. Why don't you stand up and I'll help you get the right spot?"

Melanie. *What is she doing here? I thought she escaped.*

He straightened, ignoring the taunting red cigarette glowing on the concrete patio that ran the perimeter of the building. "What the fuck are you doing here?"

"No hello for an old friend?" She arched a brow, the thin line of it truly evocative, especially when she angled a hip.

A petite five-foot-something, Melanie had curves, and a fiery attitude to match her wild, wavy hair. At times like these, when her irritation coursed unbound, Latina fire burned in her eyes and accented her words.

He shook his head. "How did they catch you?" And

why wasn't he informed? Andrew kept him apprised of most of his moves, something Wes needed given his defined role as personal guard. He used to enjoy the position of head guard at Bittech until he'd been brought over to this new place. Over here, he'd hovered in limbo since some dick called Larry already seemed to be charged with keeping the place secure.

"*What am I supposed to be doing?*" he asked as *Andrew handed him a box in his old office.*

"*Bringing this to my car.*"

"*Not the box*"—asshole—"*I mean at this new place. If that other dude is running shit, then what's my role?*"

"*You'll do whatever I tell you or else.*"

Apparently do whatever Andrew said didn't include letting Wes in on his plans for his wife.

We could easily make her a widow, his sly gator reminded.

I'm thinking about it.

Melanie deserved better.

Like us.

No. Better as in someone who wasn't a dick.

As Melanie blasted him, most of it about him being a lying sack of shit that she wouldn't piss on if he caught fire, he caught words that froze him and made him interrupt her litany of his faults.

"Rewind. What do you mean Andrew kidnapped the boys?"

"Oh, please. Don't act so innocent," she snapped. "You guys made it pretty clear last night that you're chummy. Don't tell me you don't know."

He shook his head. "I haven't seen your boys. Are you sure Andrew has them?"

Brown eyes pinned him with disdain. "Know a lot of other guys with a flying lizard on staff?"

"Which lizard?"

"Does it matter?"

As a matter of fact, it did. "That bastard. I can't believe he'd stoop to scaring his kids like that."

"Then you don't know Andrew very well," she retorted.

"Are the boys all right?"

At this query, her angry composure wavered. Her eyes filled with moisture, and she bit her lip as soon as it began to tremble. "I don't know. I have no idea how they're doing. I spent most of the night awake getting driven in loops to lose anyone who might have followed."

"Who brought you?"

"I did, of course." From around the other side of the car, an older man appeared, dressed in a suit, hair impeccably cut.

Wes knew him. Most people did. His name was Parker, and he sat as a councilor on the SHC—crooked fucker if there ever was one—oh, and a Mercer. Parker's mother had married outside the family—contrary to popular belief in town that they'd interbred.

But a different last name couldn't dilute the fact that half of Parker's DNA remained pure, bad-to-the-bone Mercer.

"I wondered when I'd see you again, Uncle."

Melanie blinked. "Uncle? You're related? I thought

I'd met all your uncles. At least those not doing time. This one is—"

"Respectable?" Wes sneered. "Only until you get to know him. Then you'll see he's just like the rest of our family."

Parker slapped a hand over his heart. "Such disdain. And for family, too. After everything I've done, I'd expect a little more gratitude."

"I'll show you gratitude. Anytime you like, you and me. No one else." The feral grin felt great.

Melanie frowned. "I'm beginning to feel like I'm in a soap opera."

"Isn't real life always a never-ending punch line?" Wes pushed away from the wall. "So where is she staying, Uncle?"

"What, aren't you going to automatically assume she'll be living with her husband?"

His lips tightened. Why did his uncle hold a taunting smirk on his lips? Had he guessed how he felt about Melanie? He'd tried very hard to hide it.

"Take me to my boys, this instant. They're the only reasons I caved to Andrew's blackmail. I want to see them now."

Distaste twisted Parker's lips. "Ah yes, the brats. I think I'll let Wes take you to them. I never could abide children. Noisy, messy things. Useless, too, until they're much older."

His uncle really deserved a smack, and Melanie seemed determined to deliver.

Wes grabbed a hold of Melanie's arms, holding her

back lest she launch herself, claws extended, at Parker's face. Knowing his uncle, that wouldn't go over well.

As she snarled and thrashed, growling, "Let me at him," he asked, "Where are the twins?"

"Tell me now or I swear I will shred you to ribbons." Melanie just might, given she managed a curled lip and a snarl, a sound no human body should ever be able to make.

Parker seemed completely unruffled by the fact she'd eviscerate him in a heartbeat. "Top floor. The new nursery unit. They're the first ones to enjoy it. But we hope to change that very soon."

For a moment, Wes stood still as a rock, despite the fact that Melanie pulled and yanked, desperate to go find her kids. Wes couldn't move because Parker's ominous words hit him with the force of a sledgehammer.

The first...implying there would be more children, yet more innocents getting drawn into the sick game his uncle and the others played.

"You can't be serious," he finally managed to mutter.

"I am. And you will not question me. Now take the woman to her brats. I've other things to attend to." With that order, his uncle stalked away.

We should eat him, too.

Except his uncle, with his tough and stringy carcass, would probably give him indigestion.

"What are you waiting for?" Melanie said, snapping him out of his paralysis. "Take me to my boys."

"I'm waiting for you to not harp."

"I don't harp. I bitch. Loudly." She eyed him with

tight lips. "So move or I'll take my ranting from mildly peeved to full-on she-bitch."

As he led the way to the building, a need to explain burned, trying to force its way past his lips. He clamped them tight. No, he wouldn't make excuses. Melanie deserved better than that.

Besides, real men didn't admit to making mistakes.

Neither did assholes.

The line between the two stretched very thin.

As they walked through the heavy metal reinforced doors that led into the research building, Melanie craned her head and let out a low whistle. "Look at the security in this place. Cameras, motion sensors, guards."

"Heat sensors, too. Also, all the doors and elevators in this place require not only a keycard but a thumbprint."

The interesting thing about the keycard was it remained clamped to a person at all times. They'd built it into the bracelets all the staff wore. Brandon, his brother, called them cuffs. But they were more than that. They were almost foolproof because they couldn't be passed along or copied. Cut the bracelet off, and as soon as it stopped touching living skin, it died—as did all that person's access.

Between that and the thumb scan, again from a living being, and the place proved impossible to navigate for any but approved personnel.

He explained that to her as they went through the security checkpoints.

"What if there's a fire or something and the electrical stops working? How would all these people get out?"

"They wouldn't."

Melanie wouldn't relent as he pressed his wrist against the scanner and then his thumb. "Surely there's some kind of back door to escape. I mean you can't convince me that Andrew and the others would rather let everyone die than have an easy way to escape."

As he yanked her into a spot before the elevators, screened by a potted plant, he leaned down and hissed, "Stop being so fucking obvious that you're looking for escape. There are eyes and ears everywhere."

"I am just showing a healthy curiosity." Her guileless appearance didn't fool.

"If you're a cat burglar casing the joint," he retorted.

"You can't blame me for wanting to leave."

"No, I can't."

The ding let him know the elevator had arrived, and he stepped out of the blind pocket, face a rigid mask, bearing straight. Let no one see the turmoil inside him.

He stepped into the cab, Melanie at his side. The doors shut, and the swipe-press combination allowed him to choose the top floor, level nine. As he stepped out and noted the bright colors, and attempt at colorful murals, he wondered if they should just rename the floor "twisted nursery."

It truly was. He'd not actually visited this floor before, assuming more offices or labs graced this level. He rarely cared to visit those. He kept his interests in the lowers levels, where they housed the experiments.

The C-shaped desk proved the island of control for a matronly woman, late fifties, her face florid, with hair scraped back in a tight bun. She wore scrubs with happy, smiling elephants, probably to counteract the scowl on her face.

"You aren't authorized for this level," said the nurse.

"I am, and so is she. This is Mrs. Killinger, the boss's wife. We understand you've got her boys here."

The flat lips of the nurse disappeared entirely in disapproval. "Indeed they are. Absolute hellions. Nothing like their father. They must have gotten the wrong side of the DNA coin toss."

The snide remark hit Melanie, but to his surprise, she didn't fly into a rage. Maturity from the firecracker he knew?

Melanie kept her eyes demurely downcast. "My boys can be a handful. If you could take me to them, I'm sure they'll calm down once they see me."

The harrumph eloquently said that Nurse Bitch didn't think so.

Since Wes had yet to release his hold on Melanie, he found himself going along, each step more horrifying for the bright flowers painted on the walls, the glimpse in rooms with glass doors, the tiny beds, empty and waiting. Too many beds. The sight of the cribs made him stumble. Melanie pulled from his grasp, face stony as she followed the nurse. He trailed more slowly.

The nurse stopped before a solid partition that required a card slide, thumbprint, and a code.

"Don't bother memorizing it," Nurse Bitch snapped as Melanie showed too much interest. "It changes every shift."

With a click, the door opened, and the nurse stepped in. Several things happened at once. Something dropped from above the door onto the nurse, something lunged at her from the floor, and amidst the screaming—lots of it comparing the twins to satanic imps escaped from hell—Melanie laughed.

"There's my good boys. Come see Mama."

Chapter 5

ONLY WHEN MELANIE HUGGED THE TWINS' small, wiry bodies did the fluttery panic, barely held at bay, subside.

My babies are okay.

They were prisoners to a sick bastard, but unharmed in body and definitely not cowed by the rabid nurse practically foaming at the mouth as she screamed, "You rotten little bastards. I don't care who your father is. You're in my domain now."

The nurse lifted a hand, but before she could use it—or lose it because Melanie would tear it off if she tried to hit her boys—Wes caught it.

"I really wouldn't do that if I were you."

The nurse tightened her lips. "I know who you are. You're Mr. Killinger's pet gator. You don't scare me."

Wes leaned close until they were almost nose to nose before he nicely, too nicely, said, "I should, seeing as how

I'm hungry, annoyed, and your antics are reminding me why being a vegetarian is overrated."

"Your kind don't eat humans." Despite her claim, the nurse pulled at the iron grip Wes had on her wrist.

"My kind eats whatever the fuck it wants, and we know how to not leave a trace behind. So, *human"*— amazing the amount of sneering he could infuse in a single word— "care to piss me off further? Go on. With the mood I'm in, it won't take much to make me snap." To emphasize his point, he noisily clacked his teeth.

The nurse wisely took a step back. A shame, because Melanie was also in a mood and wouldn't have minded seeing the bitch taken down a few more notches.

No one threatens my family. Rowr.

Head held at a haughty angle, the nurse practically spat, "Mr. Killinger and Mr. Parker will be hearing about your behavior."

"Go ahead. Do it. Tattle on me. We'll see who's more valuable to them." He winked. "I already know, so I'll bring the hot sauce for later."

"Arrrrgh." The screech of outrage lingered long after the sound of the nasty nurse's steps disappeared.

Tension eased out of Melanie, and she peeked at Wes over the heads of her boys. "Thank you."

He scowled. "Don't you dare thank me. If I hadn't put her in her place, you would have."

"And probably not as nicely." Years of trying to act the perfect mother and wife had taken their toll. Melanie could feel her Latin temper—and her inner feline— wanting to snap.

EVE LANGLAIS

"That woman is vile and shouldn't be around people, let alone children."

Taking her gaze from Wes, despite the temptation to truly drink him in, she focused on her boys. She held them out at arm's length. "Let me see you. How are you both looking?"

She twisted them this way and that, relieved at their matching eye rolls and muttered, "We're fine, Mama."

"I'll be the judge of that," she muttered because she was most definitely not.

How had her boring, cookie-cutter life gone from wake up and feed the kids breakfast before school to trying to shoot her mad scientist asshat of a husband who'd kidnapped her boys and was keeping them prisoner in what amounted to a guinea pig lab?

Since she saw no signs of injury, she lightened the moment by tickling their underarms, netting shrill giggles and shrieks. When they gasped for breath, she hugged them close again, breathing in their little-boy scent.

"Mama," said Rory, his face tucked into her shoulder, "we wanna go home. We don't like it here."

"Daddy came and said we had to be good for the lady. But I don't like her." The huffy words were spoken with a glare aimed at the empty hall.

"Never fear, I will get us out of here." Too late she remembered Wes still stood watching. Her words didn't go unchallenged.

"Don't do anything foolish. The security is absolutely stupid around here. You can't go two steps without someone knowing."

"Doing nothing would be stupider. I won't let anyone touch my boys." Vehemently said. She'd die first.

"No one's touching them. Or you."

She blinked and almost asked Wes to repeat, except he was still talking.

"Just hang tight while I work some things out."

"You want me to wait while you work some things out?" She made a face. "As if I believe you. Two minutes ago, you said there were eyes and ears everywhere. Now you want me to believe you're colluding with me to escape?"

"I wasn't lying when I said that, but I think we're safe at the moment. Look."

At his pointed finger, she turned and peeked. Then laughed.

In one corner of the large playroom, the suspended camera sported a big ball of playdough around it while, at the other end, it hung from the ceiling in a dangling mess of wires.

"Did you guys do this?" she asked her twins in a mock-stern voice.

"Not me." The identical grins brought a giggle to her lips despite the dire situation.

"There's my smart boys."

"Very smart, just like their mom. So, let me say again, I will help you. Sit tight at least for a day or two and let me figure out a way for you to escape."

"With my boys."

"Yes, with your boys."

Wes left—with a swagger she forced herself to ignore.

Why ignore? her feline wondered. Her panther had a point. The man had a nice posterior. Very nibble worthy.

But the idea of leaving teeth marks on those sweet cheeks was distracting her from the true issue, which was, should she listen to Wes and see if he could help them? *I don't know if we can afford to wait a few days.*

It didn't take a genius to see this playroom contained elements out of the ordinary, starting with a large-framed mirror she'd wager was a one-way window. People observing the kids at play, creepy, but not as creepy as the restraining straps under the tiny seats situated around tables bolted to the floor. Bars covered the windows while vents that had nothing to do with air circulation projected from the floor, the lingering scent of gas, the same kind her dentist used to knock her out, showing they'd recently tested it. *Why on earth would they need to gas children?*

And why were her boys here?

It horrified her to realize Andrew, their bloody father, had sent their boys to a lab, one with toys and games, but still another place they were doing testing. On children.

On fucking children! Snarl.

It made her stomach ill. It made her inner feline pace with bristled fur. But she couldn't let her agitation show. Mustn't let the boys sense there was something amiss, even if they already suspected.

Melanie stroked Tatum's hair back from his forehead, listening to him as he recounted a story from a picture book he'd found. Much as it chilled her, she couldn't help but wonder if it was already too late. Did some strange chemical cocktail already run through their blood?

The afternoon passed quickly and quietly. The rude nurse she'd met never reappeared. As lunchtime rolled around, a slot opened in the wall and a shelf extended with three covered trays. Sandwiches, milk, and fruit.

She sniffed them thoroughly and tasted them first, too, before she'd let her boys take a bite. Starvation wouldn't keep them strong.

Sporadically, she attempted to open the door to the room, only to find it locked each and every time. It had swung shut after Wes left, and no amount of prying, slamming, or knocking opened it.

Dinnertime arrived, and once again, food appeared, this time a meat pie with mashed potatoes and veggies. It all smelled and tasted fine, but she barely managed more than a few bites, her knotted stomach making it almost impossible to eat.

She began to wonder how long they'd have to stay here. Alone.

No one came to see them. Not Andrew. Not Wes. Not anyone.

As night fell, the sky outside the barred window darkened. She began to wonder if they'd have to sleep on the chilly tile floor.

When the door suddenly opened, she startled, and her boys, sensing her sharp spike of adrenaline and fear, tensed.

"It is time for the boys to rest." A new nurse, prim and stoic in her blue scrubs, stood in the portal. She held out her hands. "Come with me, please."

Tatum and Rory clung tight to Melanie instead. "Not going."

"Staying with Mama."

Melanie did nothing to discourage their instinct, especially since she felt the same way. As their mother, she didn't mind the weight of them sitting on and wrapped around her. That weight meant they were with her and safe.

Just try and touch them, lady.

She glared at the woman who thought she'd separate Melanie from her babies. Bared some teeth when it looked as if the nurse might lunge and try to grab one.

"What's going on here? Where is Mrs. Killinger?"

Hope fluttered in her chest. It was Wes. He'd come back.

Attention turned away from inside the room, the nurse replied, "She's in here and refusing to cooperate. I know Mr. Killinger said to use whatever force I deemed necessary, but I don't want to hurt the boys' mother in front of them. I doubt they'd be cooperative after that."

"You think?" Wes couldn't hide his disdain. "Let me handle this."

"Go ahead. Just don't hurt the subjects. They've got tests to run in the morning."

Tests? The blood in Melanie's veins froze, and she wondered if her face appeared as stricken as she felt. The wide frame of Wes, still wearing his ripped jeans from the morning, filled the doorway.

She couldn't help but whisper, "Wes, what does she mean about tests?"

"We shouldn't talk in front of little ears."

"Why not?" asked Rory.

Tugging at his lobes, Tatum frowned. "My ears aren't little."

She hugged them tightly. "I'm not leaving them."

"You're going to have to for just a little while. They aren't going to get hurt. You heard the broad. They need them." Did she imagine the curl of his lips as he repeated the nurse's words?

She kept them close as she struggled to stand. The boys had gotten so big, their bodies sturdy, and heavy. A hand under her elbow helped her get to her feet.

"Let me have one."

"No." She squeezed them closer, but Rory leaned out, arms outstretched to Wes, and said, "Carry me. On your shoulders like Luke's daddy does."

She could only blink in surprise as her son willingly went to Wes. And she blinked again as her son sat atop his shoulders.

It looked so...right? She closed her eyes and gave herself a mental shake. *Don't be casting Wes into some pathetic hero mold. And don't even start thinking about using him as a new daddy.* Even if he'd just done more in that one second of grabbing her son than Andrew had, ever.

Andrew rarely touched their boys. Very rarely. In public was about the only time the boys got away with interacting with him at all, mostly because Andrew couldn't avoid it. He cared more about the appearance of being a good father than actually trying to be one. In light of his standoffish view on parenting, she'd found it surprising he'd been talking to her about trying for another child. Looking around this place, she really wondered at his motive.

Melanie tucked her son close as she followed Wes's long stride down the hall. During the day, bright recessed lighting in the ceiling made the trek light and colorful. In the dimmer evening illumination, the flowers loomed with shadows, ominous dark spaces that implied something more evil lurked.

Not such a friendly place now.

Tucking Tatum's head close, she quickened her pace to reach the open door spilling light onto the checkered tile. She followed Wes into the bedroom. If you could call a barrack-like space with six bunk beds a bedroom.

How regimented, almost military like.

There were a few subtle differences, though. The frames of the bunks appeared of modern cappuccino-colored wood. The sheets gleamed white while fluffy comforters sporting more cheerful colors and smiling animal visages kept the feel of prisoner at bay. Barely.

A room obviously made for children, and yet, as she twirled around, she couldn't help but realize this room was meant to keep the kids locked away from everyone, including parents.

Whose kids?

Looking at her boys scrambling onto a bunk bed sporting matching comforters with ravenous dinosaurs, her heart seized.

Dear God, that bastard truly is going to experiment on his own children.

She wished she could say she harbored some hope when it came to Andrew. Some remote hope he wasn't that sick of a bastard. A foolish hope. Fathers didn't, for any fucking reason, put their kids in barracks under lock and key.

"And you condone this," she whispered.

She couldn't help but look at Wes, pained anew by his handsomeness, which obviously hid a core of bad she'd never seen before.

Funny how Wes being capable of true evil bothered her more than Andrew.

It seemed to bother Wes, too. He stood still as granite, his face a stony mask as he looked around. "I would never condone this. Never anything with children. There are some lines even I won't cross." The last words uttered at a camera in the corner of the room, a red eye blinking showing it recorded.

How she wished she could believe what Wes said. Wished she could believe the anguish in his eyes.

He's already deceived me more than once. She'd need more than words and big gator eyes to sway her into trusting him again.

"I can't leave them here," Melanie murmured, trying hard to hold in her tears. She wanted to be strong, dammit. She usually was. Anyone who knew her described her as a bomb ready to go off.

That's me. TNT. She went off on everyone except Andrew, which would probably surprise most folks. People said you fought hardest with those you loved.

Did the fact that she'd never found it in her to lambast a man who just took it and said sorry mean she didn't love Andrew?

She'd fought often with Wes.

But she'd stayed with Andrew. She bit her lip instead of tearing Andrew a new one every time he pulled away from her and the boys, especially lately as his mood had begun to swing more erratically. She couldn't help but notice the differences in her husband.

*The change in his smell...*her inner kitty slyly added.

Ah, yes, his scent. An intrinsic part of any person. The bouquet Andrew once bore had changed, gone from an earthy musk mixed with damp fur and a feel of the woods to something slightly off kilter, and if truly pressed for an answer, she would have said alien.

He's not the man he once was. Hell, Andrew had never become the man she'd hope he'd be.

Perhaps she had an unrealistic ideal. *Maybe the man I want doesn't exist.* After all, Wes couldn't seem to handle her needs either. *Am I the problem here?*

Foolish thoughts that didn't detract from the fact that her husband was seriously whacked.

And her babies were threatened.

"Get into bed, boys. Mama will tuck you in, and then I have to pop out for a little bit."

"No. Stay with us." Tatum's lower lip trembled.

"It won't be long. You'll be safe here." The lie almost stuck to her tongue. "I'm going to talk to Daddy and find out some stuff. I'll be right back."

Do I ever want to talk to him? Wes was right about one thing. Running off half-cocked wouldn't achieve anything. It certainly wouldn't help her boys, and they were her number one priority.

Tucking the blanket just below the chins on her

angels, she shivered with the righteous fury of a mother whose cubs were threatened.

If Andrew or anyone else hurts my babies, I will kill them.

Rowr.

Chapter 6

I'M GOING to have to kill Andrew.

Good. Crunch his bones. A great solution from his gator side that never liked the pompous prick.

Andrew never hid the fact he thought himself better than Wes. In his eyes, Wes was just a dumb, fucking Mercer.

A dumb, fucking Mercer that so wanted to slam his fist into the smug smirk on Andrew's face.

"Where are we going?" Melanie asked as he escorted her from the boys' room to the elevator.

"To Andrew. He asked to see you."

"Asked to see me?" She uttered a bitter laugh. "If he wanted to see me, then maybe he should have marched his lazy ass over to the prison block he's keeping our children in."

With a twitch of his finger, Wes brought her attention to the camera in the corner.

Melanie pivoted and, with a slow smile, raised not

one but two middle fingers in a salute. "I hope Andrew is watching. I hope anybody watching knows what assholes they are to be working here."

"So much for the façade of genteel lady."

"You should know by now that I might fake it, but I'll be never a lady."

The door slid open, and they stepped forth, but he waited for the pair of white-coated doctors who were babbling as they passed into the open cab before he dipped his head to whisper, "You never faked it with me."

He didn't dare pause to see her expression. He walked away wondering if she'd retort.

No, but she did reply. Her sharp kick at the back of his knee caught him off guard. He stumbled.

A laugh rumbled from him. "Still playing dirty."

"Taking advantage of your weaknesses is not dirty. It's insightful. Don't forget I know a lot of your secrets, Wes Mercer, and I will use them against you."

Good thing she didn't know his biggest secret of all.

I never got over her. Probably never would. She was the one good thing in his life. The one thing not tainted by the Mercer name. And he'd let her go.

Because she deserved better than me. She still did, but had he known she'd settle for a shithead like Andrew, then maybe he would have stuck around because he certainly wouldn't have treated her so badly. And he would have loved any kids they had. *I'd certainly never let them be brought to a place like this.*

I wish things could have turned out different. He wished he'd made different choices.

Such as now, for example. Andrew had called him

and said, "Bring me my wife," and Wes practically clicked his heels and ran to do his bidding.

He should note, however, that his haste owed less to the order and more to the anticipation of seeing Melanie again. It was bloody emasculating how a glimpse of her could brighten his day, even when she kept scowling at him.

A mate should have strength.

She's not our mate.

Yet.

Never. Because he didn't deserve her.

"How many buildings are in this compound?"

"About a half-dozen. Four of them are quarters for the staff. Another one, the two-story one, over there"—he pointed—"houses a gym facility, recreation rooms, and a variety store where you can also special order items."

"It's a prison," she observed.

"Yes." No point in denying it.

Noticing she didn't keep pace with him, he turned. She eyed him, her brow knit in question.

"You know this is a glorified prison, and yet, you seem content with it."

He rolled his shoulders. "Not so much content as resigned. I have to be here."

"Pays that good, does he?" The words daggered him with bitterness and a dose of repugnance.

"I'm not here for the money."

"Then why are you here? The guy I knew might sometimes skirt the edge of the law, but he would never be involved in something like this."

"I'm a Mercer. We're capable of anything."

"Don't you give me that line of bull. I know you and your brother Brandon at least were trying to change your reputation. To break the chain."

"Bad genes always win."

"Only if you give up."

He didn't reply. Instead, he swiped them into another building. "This is the C residence. Andrew has the entire top floor to himself." Unlike the hired lackeys, those in charge wanted for nothing.

"What about your uncle?"

"His penthouse suite is in the A building while Andrew's father is in B. The floors below them are designated to scientists, staff, and guards."

"Everyone in one place. How convenient."

More like inconvenient. Having that many people grouped meant eyes and ears everywhere on top of the cameras watching. Melanie didn't quite grasp just how under the microscope they were. She needed to stop airing her views aloud.

As soon as the elevator doors whooshed open, he yanked her in. Quick scans and a jab of his finger shut the doors, and as soon as they did, he said in a low voice. "There're no cameras in here. And before you ask, I have no idea why. I need you to listen. You can't keep ranting about Andrew and the others."

"Why not? I'm pissed, and I don't care who knows it."

"Well you should care, especially if you intend to be around for your boys."

"Is that a threat?" Her eyes sparked, and he could see the wild cat pacing behind her gaze.

"No, it's a warning. People who talk have a tendency of going missing."

"Like your brother?"

"Exactly like my brother. And others. How do you think they choose those they experiment on? Trust me when I say you don't want to become one of them."

Her lip curled. "So what are you suggesting? That I become the perfect Stepford wife?"

A snort escaped him. "As if Andrew would believe that. No, but I am saying you need to act cool. There is some strange shit going on, and when I say strange, I'm talking even more fucked up than usual. I want to help you escape. You and the boys. You don't deserve to be caught in this mess."

"No one deserves this."

The elevator jolted to a stop, but before the doors could open, he hit another floor, and it started moving again.

"I agree no one deserves the shit Bittech has put them through, but for some, it's too late."

"Is it too late for you? Are you one of their experiments?"

"Not yet, but only because they like their specimens healthy. Apparently a two-pack-a-day habit makes me ineligible. What a shame." His grin was a tad toothy, but it did bring a reluctant answering grin to her lips.

"I knew there had to be a reason for your nasty habit. So let's say I believe you when you say you're going to help me, what next?"

"You're going to have to pretend, probably for a few days—"

She interrupted. "We don't have a few days. You heard what that nurse said. They're starting on the boys tomorrow."

"Those are just the prelims. Height, weight, blood work, etc. We have time before they start."

"You've seen this before."

Wes couldn't reply as the elevator stopped. It opened and someone came on board. He and Melanie stood in silence as they went to a different floor. The stranger, with only a curious glance their way, exited.

Alone again, Wes pressed the button for the top floor. "I don't have time to explain everything. We can't stall any longer or Andrew will get suspicious. Remember what I said. Stay cool."

"I'll try."

And that was all he could truly ask for. With her cubs in danger, Melanie was a mother ready to do anything to protect. He just hoped it didn't land her locked up in the lower levels.

If it does, though, I'll find a way to bust her out.

Crunch some bones. His gator didn't mind indulging in a little violence for a good cause.

The elevator opened onto a square vestibule with a reinforced steel door facing them.

No one had access to it but Andrew. Wes put his hand on the scanner embedded in the wall, and when a female voice prompted, "Identify yourself," he said, "I brought your wife."

Not his! Snap. His inner gator couldn't help but crack its jaw at saying the word.

Andrew didn't deserve Melanie.

But neither do I.

There were clicks and the hiss of air as the door unsealed and slid sideways. Wes prodded Melanie in the back, sensing her trepidation. She straightened her shoulders as soon as she realized he'd noted her sign of weakness. Melanie always did have a strong spirit—and even stronger passion.

Remember how tight she used to hold us when we sank inside?

Nothing he did allowed him to forget. But he'd tried. Just ask his local liquor store.

Into her husband's lair Melanie stepped, the flip-flops on her feet a striking contrast to the beige Travertine stone floors. When it came to his suite, Andrew spared no luxury.

"About time you arrived, my lazy pet," Andrew called from farther inside. "I was about to send the hunters to look for you."

The hunters? A little extreme—and worrisome. Those savage creatures were more likely to rip apart their target than bring them back.

"I was tucking the boys into bed." Melanie spoke in his defense.

It irked. Wes could defend himself.

Really? Because you look like a lackey who takes shit.

And his gator looked like a pair of boots waiting to be made. The reminder of who he used to be didn't help him accept his situation, a form of slavery that involved gritting his teeth when Andrew said, "Good gator, fetching my wife. It's nice to see it's not just dogs that can learn tricks. And people said a Mercer couldn't be trained. Too dumb, they claimed. All that inbreeding, you know."

Out of habit, Wes clamped his lips tight. But Melanie didn't know Andrew did this on a regular basis, taunted him constantly in the hope of making him snap.

Hands planted on her hips, Melanie wouldn't let it slide. "Leave Wes and his family alone. He did what you asked. No need to insult him."

Andrew stood from his chair, and Wes recognized the glint in his eye, the mad one that appeared more and more frequently. "Are you defending him? Do you still have feelings for your high school sweetheart, dear wife?"

"Of course not. You should know me well enough by now to know I won't listen to you degrade someone. What surprises me is the fact I even have to say this to you. You never used to treat people this way."

"Perhaps I got tired of the so-called stronger predators treating me as if I was inferior." Andrew's lip curled in a sneer. "Now I am the one with all the power, and it's time to pay them back for some of their taunts."

Some people never got over the hierarchy from school. As a bit of a nerd, a rich one with a snooty attitude, Andrew tended to get shoved into a fair number of lockers. Wes knew he'd done it a time or two. Maybe more. Stolen Andrew's lunch, too, every Wednesday. That was roast beef sandwich day. Wes enjoyed every bite of that juicy meat on the fresh Kaiser layered with provolone cheese, a touch of mustard, and lettuce.

Wes leaned against the wall by the elevator, prepared to listen to Andrew's spiel about how mean people were.

"Don't bother getting comfortable, gator. The wife

and I are going to have a chat. *Alone*. You may leave. I'll contact you when I need you again."

Bite his fucking face off.

His gator didn't like Andrew's attitude, and neither did he. But he also hated more the idea of leaving Melanie alone with the prick. His fists clenched at his sides. How he longed to lunge at the man—*bite his head off*. The crunch would sound so good. Yet, it would achieve nothing.

It would make me feel much better. His gator had no doubt.

We can't eat him. Not yet, not while Andrew and Uncle Parker held all the cards.

It irked another had that kind of power over him. Even worse, the guy with the power showed signs of madness, a side effect of the drugs he'd helped create and then imbibed.

Everything came at a cost. Andrew had gained great strength from the drugs he took, but he'd lost something else. All his marbles. Only a few seemed left rolling around. Anyone could see the growing madness in his eyes.

But Wes couldn't do anything about it yet.

We mustn't leave the female with him.

What if Andrew tried to hurt Melanie?

Chomp him if he dares!

And what of the others he had to also protect?

As if sensing his dilemma, she cast a glance over her shoulder. She didn't speak aloud, but her eyes said, "Go," and she mouthed, *I'll be fine.*

"Is there a problem?" Andrew asked.

Yeah. The fact that Andrew still breathed. He tamped down those words and instead forced out, "No problem, boss. I'm going to have a smoke, so if you need me, I won't be far."

A leer stretched Andrew's features. "Don't come running if you hear screams. The wife is a noisy thing."

I know, you fucking prick. He couldn't fucking forget. And the bastard poked at the memory wound.

Because he's a prick. Prick. Prick. The word repeated itself over and over as Wes stalked from Andrew's apartment and back into the elevator. His anger ran higher than usual after a session with his boss.

No denying the guy deserved an award for his extreme asshole persona, but Andrew deserved to die the most for having the legal right to be with Melanie every day.

I would give anything to be in his shoes and sleep beside her.

Sleep? his gator grunted. *A true bull does better things than just sleep beside his female.*

A smart male would do such dirty things to Melanie... Dirty, sweaty, fun things.

Things only Andrew could do! S*nap.*

But didn't. The loser.

Wes didn't understand it. How could Andrew have a woman like her, a freaking amazing spitfire of a woman, and not treat her like a queen? Andrew should worship her. Instead, he treated Melanie like shit.

We should go back for a chat. Just open our mouth and—

No eating him until I know I can get everyone out safe.

He wouldn't abandon anyone to this fate. And, no, that didn't make him a fucking hero. Perish the thought. Wes just didn't like assholes, which might explain why there were days he didn't like himself.

It killed him to leave her behind, killed him knowing that Melanie had to deal with Andrew alone, but he couldn't tip his hand too soon.

I need a cigarette. Instead of going down to the lobby, he jabbed a button to go one level down.

His keycard and thumb allowed him to open the door at the end of the hall and take the sturdy metal stairs two at a time. Then three.

Within him, a wildness burned and churned. Restlessness tore at him. Break out. Get free. Can't.

Fuck.

He slammed into the bar for the outer door and burst out onto the rooftop. He stopped dead in the crisp evening air, arms spread wide, head tilted. He sucked in a deep breath, trying to tame the wildness.

Need to find a quiet fucking place in my mind. He needed to calm himself. Concentrate on something else.

The dark sky greeted him, along with a roof deck that, while spotted with structures for venting, offered a lot of open space. In an attempt to remain green, they'd actually laid grass down, soft and downy. In an effort to save it from nasty smokers, at the far end, they'd built a gazebo, with benches bolted under it and ashtrays.

Best of all, it was far from cameras. Far from the door he wanted to barrel back through. He wanted to go back and take Melanie from Andrew. And kill the man if he stood in his way. Instead, a long stride brought him to the other end of the roof deck.

A hard jolt as he hit the bench made it creak. Nothing like some rude furniture to remind a guy he would never be a lightweight.

The cigarette emerged from his pocket, and in a moment, his lighter ignited with a dancing flame. He put the cigarette between his lips, clamping the fresh paper covering the filter. He sucked in, tugging air through the tip. A rush of warm smoke flowed into him, and his eyes closed as his head tilted back.

That's the rush I needed.

Non-smokers never understood the appeal. *All you're doing is inhaling smoke. Big deal*, they said. The health effects weren't worth it. All true, and yet, he'd admit to a certain guilty euphoria every time he lit one. He knew smoking was bad for him. Knew he shouldn't do it. But he did it anyway.

He sucked in that smoke, held it for a second, and exhaled. In and out, the relaxing mantra—a huge part of smoking relaxed him. Tension eased from his stiff frame, and for a moment, he didn't feel as if he'd explode.

Then his brother Brandon, who'd arrived with his usual stealth, spoke. "Tough day at the office?"

He cocked open an eye. "Aren't they all? This not smelling thing is really freaking me out. Are you wearing that damned cologne they're testing again?"

"Eau de nothing? Yeah. They've got it working, as you noticed, but it doesn't last more than a few hours. They're trying to extend it."

"That's not the only thing they're doing," Wes muttered. "Did you know they were moving on to testing with kids?"

Not a single twitch of surprise on his brother's face. "Did Uncle finally tell you?"

"He didn't have to. I saw it for myself. Why the fuck didn't you tell me?"

"This is the first chance we've had to talk since your arrival."

"Things have gotten so fucked up."

Brandon snorted. "As if they weren't already."

"Oh yeah, well, get this. Andrew's got his own kids living on the top floor of the lab in that weird freaking nursery he's got going. His kids, for fuck's sake."

"I'd hoped they would escape." Brandon sighed, and there was a leathery rustle as he shifted in the shadows. "Andrew is toppling into the abyss of madness. I think our uncle is, too."

Toppling? More like already ankle deep in shit in it. "How's your mind doing?" Wes asked.

A wry grin pulled at Brandon's face, crinkling it. "I'm mostly in control of it now, but it's a battle. There's a new voice in my head, and he's a cold fucking bastard. So don't forget your promise to me."

As if Wes could considering how Brandon had begged. *If I go mad, you have to kill me before I cause harm.*

The things a man had to promise family. Wes looked down rather than at his little brother, a prisoner of Bittech because of what they'd done to him.

"I remember what I said. No need to remind me."

Because he hoped to never have to do it. "Unless you're trying to tell me something. Is this your way of saying you need a tail-whooping?"

"Anytime, big brother, anytime."

Neither of them moved, the ritual of words an old one. Wes ground out the cigarette in the mounted ashtray and immediately lit another.

"Those things aren't good for you," Brandon said.

"I know. The damned nicotine keeps showing in my urine tests, and I keep my job. Bernie, on the other hand, along with Judd, they weren't so lucky. None of the other shifter guards have had any luck recently. They're all gone. Is it me, or are the guards they're using all human mercenaries for hire now?"

"Saw that, too, did you? I didn't clue in until we got here. The missing shifter guards are being held in the new holding facility."

A polite term for they were the newest Bittech test subjects. "What floor are they keeping them on?" Wes asked, the smoke highlighting his words.

"Below ground. And highly secured. I thought for sure after what happened to Merrill I'd wake up in there."

"But?" Wes pushed, knowing the cameras didn't extend this far from the stairwell.

Brandon rolled his wide shoulders. "But what? I guess when they found me passed out on the ground they figured I was a victim. No one has said anything about suspecting I helped those others escape or that I turned on Merrill."

"So you're in the clear."

"I guess. For now."

"I think if they suspected, we wouldn't be talking now. And who's left to betray you?" No one, and it was hard for dead bodies to talk. See, Brandon had tried his best to aid some of the captives in fleeing their prison. Key word being tried.

All of the attempts had failed but for one. The only escapee who'd made it out successfully had been Aria, and as soon as she did speak, Bittech shut down and relocated.

"At least that prick Merrill is finally dead," Brandon announced with a bit of glee.

About time, too. He was another guy who'd taken the Bittech cocktail and found himself with a few loose screws.

"Way I heard it, Constantine got a little peeved when they took his girl from him." And snapped Merrill's neck like a twig.

I can't think of a more deserving punishment.

"The man is a beast."

No, Constantine was a python with a penchant for hugs. Constantine was also one of the good guys. "And off-limits. We're damned as it is. Let's not start adding the death of decent folk to it."

"I don't hurt my friends," Brandon hissed, in better control these days of his rolling S problem. "I'm not fucking crazy."

"Yet."

"Yet. So don't piss me off, or you'll be first on my shit list."

"What do you mean first, you prick? Shouldn't that slot be reserved for Andrew? Or our dear uncle?"

"They've only tortured me for a few years. You, on the other hand, started the day I was born." Brandon smiled, not the human smile he was born with.

"You needed it. I toughened you up. It's a fucked-up world out there. You gotta be strong to survive it."

"Some days I'd rather just say screw it."

"Never give up, brother. Never give up."

Because, if a man couldn't believe in redemption, then what was the point of living?

Chapter 7

WITH WES GONE, Melanie found herself alone with Andrew, suffering a trepidation she'd never felt before around her husband. She couldn't help but recall his new strength. Would he use it against her?

If he tries, we'll claw him good.

Except, she still couldn't seem to manage to draw out her cat.

A cat that now sulked at the reminder she was stuck.

"Alone at last," Andrew announced with all too much glee. His smile too wide. His teeth too many.

To distract herself from Andrew, and his oddly frightening expression, she glanced around the space. There was certainly a lot of it, and richly appointed, too.

Hardwood floors gleamed from one end to the other, covered in thick shag rugs in varying shades of gray. Strategically placed modern furniture with lots of glass, chrome, and odd art pieces defined the various areas.

A massive bed, which made her stomach roil, took up

one entire corner. Across from it sat a matching leather couch and club seat arrangement in front of a huge television screen. Look at that. It sported a game console underneath, but she'd bet it wasn't there for the boys.

As she kept pivoting to take in details, she couldn't help but see her husband, a husband who looked markedly different. For one, his face appeared bare. Without his glasses, Andrew's eyes looked small. Sly. He held himself a tad straighter in his comfortable name-brand athletic pants and matching shirt. No off-the-rack bargain items for him. He was very finicky that way.

Realizing he was the center of her regard, Andrew swept an arm. "Welcome, dear wife, to your new home."

She shook her head. "I had a home. A nice one that I decorated myself. You know, the one with a room for the boys." Funny how she used to hate the cookie-cutter neighborhood with its bland sameness, but now missed it something terrible. That house represented normalcy. This place however? While large, it definitely was not designed to be kid, or even wife, friendly. For all intents and purpose, it appeared as a bachelor pad.

The realization worried. She got the impression Andrew had this place tailor-made. If that were the case, then the omissions for his family were intentional, and it meant Andrew no longer felt a need to maintain a pretense of being a family man. She didn't know what else to conclude because, otherwise, he would have included in the design quarters with an extra bedroom for the kids.

The fact that he never intended to have the boys live

here bothered her, and it also brought another realization to the forefront.

If he's willing to abandon his children, then what will he do to me?

Tread carefully. This one is dangerous.

She didn't need her feline's warning to recognize the potential for ugliness in her current situation. She wasn't dealing with the man she'd married. This new pacing Andrew exuded a weird kind of energy. She could almost see it humming inside him, practically bursting to get out.

The cracked mirror on a far wall made her wonder if his control had slipped already.

He's going mad.

And Wes left her alone to deal with it.

Some might say give the guy some slack. He'd dropped her off to see her asshat of a husband. She said no way. Real men didn't deliver a woman to someone with a mad glint in their eye.

Then again, lily-kneed husbands didn't usually turn into borderline lunatics.

"What's going on, Andrew?" With no sure option, she chose the direct approach.

"What's going on? Why, the beginning of a new era, one where we can all be strong." Andrew flexed his arm, and the muscle in it did a sickly ripple.

"You experimented on yourself?" She couldn't help a horrified lilt to her query.

"It's not experimentation if it's proven beneficial."

But she cared less about what he'd done to himself than what he planned to do with their sons. "Why have you brought Rory and Tatum here?"

"Can't a father want to be with his family?" The toothy smile sent a shiver down her spine.

"You've never shown an interest before."

"Because before I never had a use for them. At the time, they were too young."

"Too young for what?"

The creepy grin widened. "You'll see."

Screw not saying anything and staying cool as Wes advised. Wes wasn't here, and someone threatened her boys.

"No, I don't see. I don't understand how you could think it was all right to experiment on children."

"When it comes to great scientific breakthroughs, risks must be taken."

"Some of those risks have proven deadly. Look at all those who've died."

"Unfortunate casualties."

She blinked as he continued to blow off all the things he'd done. The things he planned to do.

I made a mistake in coming here. I won't be able to reason with him. She should return to the boys and keep watch over them until she could fabricate a plan for them to escape. Despite Wes's reassurance, she couldn't wait. She didn't dare wait.

Turning on her heel, she headed back to the door, only to hear Andrew snap, "Where do you think you're going?"

"Away from you."

"You won't get far without this."

Whirling, she was just in time to catch the envelope he tossed at her.

"While you're acting very bitchy, I've been a wonderful husband preparing you this wondrous apartment, and look at the bracelet I got you. Go on. Pull it out."

Fingers trembling, she pulled the tab on the envelope, the rip of paper loud in the silence between them. She shook out a bracelet, heavy gold and metal, embedded with garish bling.

"I spent a fortune on it. Put it on."

She didn't want to. It reminded her too much of the shackles keeping her here, in this compound, with this lunatic.

But it might be the key to our escape.

Swallowing back the sour taste in her mouth, she clamped the cold bracelet around her wrist, trying not to wince as it clicked shut.

"Behave and you'll have free run of most of the compound."

"And if I don't?"

"I wouldn't recommend it. Now, aren't you going to come here and thank me for my generosity? Parker thought you'd be too difficult to deal with and wanted to put you in a cage."

Her eyes widened, and shock kept her from speaking.

Andrew's face hardened. "But I reminded him that you were my business. *Mine.* I decide what happens to you. Me!"

Given his vehement response, it probably wasn't a good time to declare she wanted a divorce.

Death would be faster.

And probably more satisfying, except she currently

was at a disadvantage. No kitty popping out meant no chance against Andrew.

Thank for the reminder that I'm stuck. Her kitty went off to pout again.

It just added to the surreal moment. She needed to escape before the scream building within her unleashed.

"I have to go."

"So soon? Why?"

Would Andrew take offense if she said she needed to get away from him because he'd obviously gotten a bit of loon in whatever drugs he'd taken? "I have to go check on the boys."

"No need to leave. They're fine. See?" Andrew aimed a remote at the television, and it blinked from an aquarium scene to a room lit in bright green.

She took a step forward, jaw dropping at the sight. "You're spying on our kids?"

"I prefer to think of it as keeping an eye on the investment."

"They're not lab rats, you bastard. They're your children."

He arched a brow. "Are you sure of that?"

He did not. Oh yes he did.

"Are you implying I slept around? You know I was never unfaithful. Those babies might have come from a tube, but they're still a part of both of us."

Andrew shook his head. "That's where you're wrong, wife. They're not mine at all."

The roaring white noise in her ears didn't let her hear if he said anything more. What more could he say? He'd just taken her world and turned it upside down.

If Andrew spoke the truth, and the boys weren't his, then were they even hers? She should have stayed and asked, but she couldn't. Couldn't bear to hear more of his vile truths.

Blinded by his words, she somehow stumbled from Andrew's presence and managed to make her way to the ground floor. She staggered from the elevator, ignoring the curious glances of those waiting to grab it.

Air. I need air. She bolted for the front doors, bursting out into the crisp evening. She sucked in a heavy lungful, but it didn't clear the taint from her lungs. All of her being was tainted with Andrew's revelation. As she leaned against the building outside, she reeled, and her breath came in short, panicked pants.

What if the boys aren't mine?

Furry slap. Her feline growled. *Those are our cubs.* The boys, no matter what DNA ran in their veins, were Melanie's in every way that counted. She'd carried them, birthed them, changed their poopy asses, and bandaged their cuts.

They are mine.

Her cat snorted and then took a big, exaggerated sniff. It hit Melanie.

Their scent. How could she forget the fact that her little tykes smelled feline and were the spitting image of Daryl at that age? How could she have doubted for even a second. *They are my flesh and blood.* No ifs, ands, or buts about it.

Yet, if Andrew told the truth and he hadn't contributed the other half, then who provided the male gene to her sons?

Who is their true daddy?

"You shouldn't be out here."

A scream got caught in Melanie's throat, and she pushed against the hard wall at her back. She blinked at the lizard man that drifted to the ground on leathery wings.

What a strange sight. Sure, she'd heard about the flying dinomen plaguing town, but to see one in person? Seeing one also made her wonder, *did I get the sane or crazy lizard?* An answer that would determine her chances for survival.

Because, according to sources, there were two—the one that wouldn't hesitate to tear a man to pieces and the one who seemed to want to be on their side.

Please don't let it be the killing lizard.

Wings pulled tight against its back, jutting in a tall peak over the shoulder. The man, with scaled skin and alien features, cocked his head. "You shouldn't be outside. There are monsters about."

You don't say. An urge to giggle clenched her teeth tight, and taking a deep breath, she managed to mutter, "Are you going to kill me?"

Very human eyes stared from the reptilian face. "Depends. Are you going to try and kill me?"

Given he towered over her and had big teeth and claws? "Probably not." She remembered enough to know a touch of his claws or tongue and he'd inject enough paralytic poison to incapacitate her.

"Then we both shall live another day. Pity."

He sounded quite put out about the whole surviving part. "Who are you?"

"Ace. I work here." As he explained, he tugged the collar around his neck. Ringed and seamless in appearance, she'd heard enough from Renny to know Bittech used them to command the shifters, using pain as their whip.

A crappy thing to do. And yet, despite that, it hadn't stopped one of those guys from trying to do the right thing.

"Are you the guy who helped Cynthia's friend, Aria?"

A slight flare of his nostrils and a smidgen of wider eyes. Melanie could see his lips mouth the word no, a word Ace orated aloud. "No. Not me. The bird flew the coop on her own."

He lied. But why? It took her only another second to remember the cameras. Shit.

I really need to remind myself I'm on a sick version of reality television where my every move and word is watched.

Not saying anything, though, would appear suspicious. Surely some basic discourse was allowed. She couldn't exactly nod and smile all the freaking time. She started with an obvious question.

"Were you always like this?" The query shamed her almost the moment it left her lips.

How rude of her to assume he suffered a deformity. Perhaps he enjoyed his hybrid shape. Half-man in shape, with two legs and arms. He wore clothing, pants and a shirt, which seemed at odds with other reports that claimed they wore nothing.

"And its balls and man thing are hidden," Renny confided.

"Then how could you know it's a male?" Melanie queried as she used nail polish remover on the marker on the wall.

"You can tell."

Renny proved correct. No mistaking Ace for anything less than male. And he seemed familiar somehow.

He also answered her question before she could recant it.

"Are you asking if I was born a monster?" The lips turned down on the reptilian face, a human mannerism that made him seen less alien. "It doesn't really matter now, does it? I know what people see when they look at me, and there is nothing I can do to change it."

Such sadness in those words. "Maybe doctors could..." Her sentence halted.

With a coil of his hind legs, Ace leaped into the air, unfurling mighty wings with a canvas snap. The wings caught an air stream. They filled and let him soar above. With a hard sweep, he shot higher before banking and flying out of sight.

The night returned to its normal silence. The playing of a radio from somewhere, the occasional sharp bark of laughter as some people went about their lives as if they weren't all fucked.

Like totally fucked.

How am I going to get myself and my babies out of here?

Climb. There wasn't a fence that existed she couldn't

scale. Her cat had no doubt they could do it, yet what of her little ones? They couldn't move into their cat self yet. They were agile, and fearless. However, they would be limited by their age and their bodies.

But I can't leave without them.

The dilemma burned. *I'm their mother. I'm all they have. I have to fix this.* She wasn't so desperate, though, as to not realize she needed help.

Daryl would move heaven and earth for her in a second if she asked. Maybe she could get to a phone and call him.

And how will he know where to go?

Good question since she hadn't the slightest clue where they were. When she'd obeyed Andrew's instructions to come, she'd obeyed all too well. She'd been handed a hood, and worn it, trying not to panic under the material. She also tried to not blow a fuse until she found her boys. There was a time and place for anger. And when she did unleash her anger, it would leave a river of pain.

Leave no enemy breathing.

No enemy indeed, she silently promised from under that hood. Parker meant to take away her power but, instead, wound up making her stronger. Although he had achieved one thing. She'd gotten completely, utterly lost. The car appeared to turn and turn again during the ride to the new Bittech compound with Parker.

So what exactly would she say to Daryl if she did call him? *Hey, big bro, so I'm like in this place, a big place with like buildings and people, lots of people with guns, oh and a fence. A big fence. With like woods around it. Under a sky.*

Could she get any more freaking vague?

Don't waste a phone call until you have an actual pinpoint on your location. Thinking of pinpoint, she could have slapped herself. A cell phone could map her location.

Next question: who to get the cell phone from?

She heard the whoosh and click of a door opening then shutting. She remained leaning against the wall of the building.

"What are you doing out here?"

It didn't surprise her to see Wes appear. Everywhere she turned these days, she ran into him. "Funny you should ask because Ace just asked the same thing."

At the mention, he stiffened. "You met Ace? You talked to him?"

"Only for a moment." She turned and fixed her gaze on him. "You know him?"

"Yeah."

"He's not what I expected. He didn't kill me."

"That would be because Ace isn't like the others. He hasn't let the treatments drive him to madness. But that doesn't mean you should trust him."

"Then who am I to trust then? It seems I can't rely on you. Or have you forgotten you're the one who tried to bring me here in the first place? Let's also not forget the fact you're Andrew's lap pet."

He stiffened. "I'm not his bitch."

"Perception is everything, though, and from where I'm standing, you are just as dirty as him." She took a step away, aiming herself in the direction of the medical facility that housed her sons.

Wes kept pace. It shouldn't have pleased her.

"Go away," she snapped.

"I'm not leaving you. The monsters are off their leash tonight. It's not safe."

"You don't say, seeing as how I'm being escorted by a monster right now."

"They didn't experiment on me."

"Well la-di-da for you. What about everyone else?"

His lips tightened. "Who do you trust that you can call for help?"

"Are you asking for people who might look for me? Looking to grab them, too? Make some monsters out of the people you know?"

"I'm not the enemy. I want to help you." He tried to grab at her, but she danced out of reach.

"Don't you touch me," she snapped.

"I know you hate me right now, but you need to calm the fuck down."

"Or you'll what? What can you possibly do to me that would be worse than this hell I'm living already?"

"I don't want to make shit worse. I want to make it better. Which is why I am asking you to give me a name so I can get your ass out of here. Who should I call? Your brother, Daryl? What about that uncle you've got living in Tampa?"

She whirled, and her hands shot out at him, pushing at his hard chest, trying to shove him back. What she really wanted to do involved shoving all her frustration and anger somewhere the sun never shone.

76

"No. No. And no. I can't call anyone, dammit, not Daryl, not my uncle. No one. I can't risk their lives. I won't have them suffer because my husband is a madman."

This mess with Andrew is my problem. My responsibility.

But she couldn't say that out loud, and hitting Wes felt good. She even yelled a bit as she kept pummeling at him. And he let her, let her wail and scream and hit and cry until eventually she collapsed against him. Her breath came in stuttering hitches, and her eyes burned with hot tears she couldn't shed.

Don't cry. Crying is for pussies.

We are a pussy.

He wrapped his arms around her and held her tightly. He didn't say a word. The best thing he could have done because there were no words to make this better, no words to make things right.

Although he did find three that managed to warm her for a moment.

"I'll kill him."

Chapter 8

"I'LL KILL HIM."

Yes, he'd said those words. Out loud. While Andrew's wife—*the woman I want*—was listening.

Most women would have received his claim one of two ways. Exclamations of happiness and calling him their hero.

Others, knowing of the Mercer reputation for violent solutions, would have recoiled and screamed.

What did his sweet Latina do? Melanie laughed. And laughed. Snorted, too.

Absolutely adorable. But totally at his expense. "Why are you laughing?"

"Because that is a load of crap. I will kill him," she mocked in a low voice. "As if. You were the one who told me there are cameras outside. No way are you going to say something like that on live feed unless it's a ploy to get me to trust you. Not happening."

"This is not a ploy," he snapped. He'd noted the pair

of crushed cameras on their walk over to the science lab building. One of them littered the ground in a pile of plastic and wires. The other had left only the mounting brackets behind.

Something hating technology had passed this way, meaning there was a blind spot in the system—and an angry predator loose.

Melanie evaded his grasp and sprinted to the door of the building. She ran her wrist on the scanner and then squashed her thumb.

"Andrew gave you security access?"

She held up her arm. "Yes. Gaudy, isn't it? Apparently he wants to try and make things work."

"And do you?"

"You only get one chance to fuck me over." She yanked the door shut, sealing it, and moved away, but he could still see her through the glass.

He should have turned around and walked away at that point. Just point his feet in the other direction and go.

Yeah, who was he fucking kidding? There was only one place he wanted to go. He swiped his wrist and pressed his thumb on the scanner. The door hissed open on its mechanical track.

He strode in and then through a second set of doors manned by a guard who only briefly looked up from behind his bulletproof glass.

Layers and layers of security. A place meant to ensure no escapes—at least none that were alive.

Wes caught up to Melanie at the elevators, where she waited with arms crossed In the blind spot, in a low voice, he resumed their conversation from outdoors. "It won't happen again." All too aware of the cameras in the ceiling, he kept his words neutral and hoped she'd get the hint.

A sneer lifted her lip, but on this fiery Latina, it served only to heighten her appearance. The Melanie he remembered always showed her every emotion on her face.

And the emotion expressed right now was anger. She stomped into the elevator and opened her mouth. He punched the camera before she launched in on him.

"Aren't you a big, brave man now, hurting a poor, defenseless camera? Afraid management will find out what you say behind their back? And I mean say because, if you ask me, someone in this place took your balls or else you would have acted a long time ago."

Ouch. She knew how to hit a man with words. "I never condoned what they did."

"But you sat by and watched. Fuck, you even led the whole gang on about it. What was that about? Telling Daryl and Caleb and Constantine that you think something is whacky at Bittech; meanwhile, you know there is. Hell, you had access to it."

He should have realized she'd eventually remind him of his subterfuge with Caleb and the rest. She thought he'd done it to garner info. The reality was he'd started the rumors and then kept feeding them in the hope someone without their hands tied could act. Then again, though, if the SHC couldn't ride to the rescue of those caught by Bittech, then who could? One lone gator was no match for the perfidy he'd encountered.

I could have done more to lead them to the atrocities. But at what cost? If Wes got caught, he wasn't the one who would suffer most.

What he could do was apologize. It almost made his gator death roll in shame. "What I did was wrong. I won't deny that. Just like I won't deny I'd do it again. I wouldn't have a choice."

"We all have choices. I chose to marry a douchebag. You chose to work for him. One is easy to walk away from. The other is going to need a good divorce lawyer."

"I can't walk away. And I think you know by now you can't either."

The doors slid open for the top level, and he glanced through them to see the nurse behind her station eyeballing them with curiosity.

He slapped the door-close button. "For now, at least, I have to stay and do as I'm told."

"Waiting for a final paycheck before you run?"

Dammit, he was tired of her accusations. Tired of her thinking he was just like Andrew.

I'm nothing like that bastard. He had reasons for what he did. And perhaps it was time he stopped hiding them. "I can't run until I find out where Parker's hidden my baby sister."

Chapter 9

THERE WERE times in a person's life when you felt like a jerk. The time you borrowed your best friend's last tampon and didn't replace it and her period came early. When you shortchanged the waitress at a diner on her tip because you forgot your debit card and didn't have quite enough cash.

Then there was accusing a man of being a total douchebag, only to find out he acted as he did because of his little sister.

He did it to help his family.

Dammit. Melanie's back hit the wall of the elevator, and with it bracing her, she slid to the floor.

I'm such an awful bitch. She'd accused Wes of doing this because he wanted to, but like her, he had to. They both did for those they loved.

Wes balanced on the balls of his black boots as he crouched before her. "Are you okay?"

"No. I don't think I'll ever be okay," she said in a half-sob. "This is a freaking nightmare, and I just want to wake up." The bottom of her hand hit the floor in a fisted thump.

"Shit's pretty bad right now."

"Pretty bad?" She eyed him with a wry grimace. "We're being held prisoner by men who think nothing of holding children as hostages against us. How much worse can it get?" At the bleak expression he got in his eyes, she held up her hands. "Wait. Don't tell me. I don't think I want to know."

"Things are escalating. We need to escape."

"You have a plan?" She turned a hopeful gaze on him.

His lips pulled taut. "No. Not yet. A lot of this security was put in place without me. I don't have the same freedom of movement that I had previously. No one does."

"Are you saying you can't leave?"

He shook his head. "If I get anywhere near the fence, my bracelet jolts. If I keep going, a guard finds me and asks me what the fuck I'm doing."

"That's a little emasculating, don't you think? A human asking you to go back to your room and be a good boy?"

"Are you seriously mocking me?"

She shrugged. "Someone has to." *Because a true predator would eat any human that dared to cage them as a snack. Crunch.*

Oops, she might have said that out loud because Wes laughed.

"The problem with eating guards is those damned

buttons on their shirts tend to get caught in the teeth"—he grinned wide as she gasped—"of my wood chipper."

She punched him. "You jerk. You tried to make me think you really are a man-eater."

"Not yet, but lately I've been tempted."

It reminded her why Wes was as much a prisoner as she was. "Which of your sisters did Parker take and hide?"

"The youngest. Sue-Ellen."

"And you haven't gotten her released yet?" Even though she didn't say it, the unspoken words hovered in the air between them. *And you expect me to believe you can help me?*

He explained. "The reason I haven't taken off is because only Uncle Parker knows where she is, and he's not telling. She's his leverage to get me and Brandon to behave."

"Wait, Brandon's here, too? I thought he was missing. That's what everyone in Bitten Point said."

Wes sighed. "I've been saying lots of shit to keep their fucking secret. I was warned that, if I didn't, they'd do something to my family." He shrugged. "I'm their brother. I did what I had to."

"Oh, Wes."

"Don't give me that look, angel." The old nickname slipped from him and hung in the air.

She glanced to the side, breaking the eye contact. She had to find her equilibrium.

The futility of the situation made a tear slip and run hotly down her cheek. A rough thumb wiped at it.

"Don't cry. Don't you dare fucking cry. You know I hate it when you do."

The words served only to make more hot tears roll. Two. Three. He wiped each and every one, except for the one that made it to the corner of her mouth.

That one he kissed away. Awareness exploded at the gentle touch, and she inhaled sharply. She didn't move, couldn't as his hands cupped her cheeks and he continued to kiss her, exploring her mouth with slow sensuality.

Tasting her. Savoring her. Igniting the senses she thought dulled.

He reminded her what it felt to be alive. To be a woman. To...

"No." She pushed away from him, and he let her go, the ease of her escape a frustration to go with that of her burning lips and aching body.

She liked the touch of Wes against her. Her body wanted more.

Rub against him. Skin to skin.

"We can't do this," she whispered, her voice husky and low. "It's wrong."

"You're right. We shouldn't do this, but the problem is it's right. You know it feels right."

More right than anything other than her sons right now. But thinking of her sons reminded her she wasn't a free woman. Married women, even unhappy ones, did not make out with ex-boyfriends in elevators.

"Don't do that again." She rose to her feet and needed a hand against the wall of the elevator to steady herself.

Rising more slowly, Wes towered over her, but she

wouldn't look at him. Instead, she reached around his broad bulk and jabbed the door-open button. She ducked under his arms as they swished apart. "Goodnight, Wes."

He didn't reply. He didn't follow.

Why doesn't he chase me?

Melanie itched to turn around and see what he felt. See if he cared.

The doors swished shut, and the elevator hummed as it left.

Wes had left. It hurt more than it should have, which meant she was in no mood for the nurse who tried to get in her way.

"This wing is for the children only."

Oh, hell no. You chose the wrong night to play dominant with me.

Melanie raised her gaze to pin the nurse with laser-hot eyes. "If you want to keep your throat intact, then you will not get between me and my sons."

The nurse might have a few pounds on Melanie, but she had enough wits to realize who would emerge the victor.

Just in case the other woman needed reminding that she dealt with a predator, as Melanie strode the length of the hall, she strained hard enough to pop some claws—finally some success!—and she dragged them along the wall. The sound proved exceptionally delightful, given the painted murals cleverly covered the metal-plated walls.

Screech. She hoped that sound haunted the nurse's dreams.

Chapter 10

AFTER A SLEEPLESS NIGHT, Wes found himself outside on the quad, leaning against a tree, a cigarette clamped between his lips.

For the first time in a long while, the acrid smoke did not calm him. Nothing could calm him, not while Melanie was here.

In danger.

Fuck.

Even worse? He didn't know what he could do to help her.

Double fuck.

But at least his visit the previous evening to his uncle's apartment had given him that hope.

Parker opened his door and arched a brow at seeing him. "A little late to be visiting, don't you think?"

Pushing past his uncle, Wes entered the richly appointed suite, noting that, like Andrew, his uncle had spared no expense when it came to his accommodations.

Unlike Andrew's open loft concept, his uncle had gone with a more traditional layout, with the foyer opening onto the living area and the bedroom hidden from view.

"We need to talk about Andrew's plan to experiment on his kids."

"Andrew's plan?" His uncle shut the door and strode past him. "Is he taking the credit for my idea?"

Could a gator's blood run any colder? "You mean this is your doing? What the fuck is wrong with you? You're talking about screwing with kids."

"Think of them more as our bright future." Stopping before a sideboard sporting several glass decanters with amber-hued and other tinted booze, his uncle poured himself a drink in a snifter. He brought it to his nose and sniffed. "Ah, nothing like a good bourbon." He took a sip. "Perfection. But I should mention not all bourbons are made equal. Just like not all shifters are made the same. Some are strong. Some can fly. So many traits that, when separate, make us unequal. However, let's say you could blend some of those into everyone. What if we took away the barriers and gave everyone the ability to fly?"

Wes couldn't help a snort. "You are not doing this to be altruistic. As if you'd let anyone get that strong."

A grin twisted his uncle's thin lips. "How well you know me, nephew. You're right. I don't think everyone should have this power. This strength. But for the right sum, it can be done."

The fact that his uncle did it for money wasn't new to Wes. Parker didn't do anything for free. "Your money-making scheme isn't a reason to start experimenting on children."

"That's where you're wrong. See, the researchers believe that some of our epic failures are because our test subjects were too old. You might have noticed that only the most strong-willed retain their sanity. The most alpha, I guess you could say. Their theory for that is quite simple. The addition of more animal genes creates a schism in the mind. Too many thoughts in one place. So they devised a theory. What if those genes were blended into the DNA structure of a child before their beast emerges? What if we could stop the madness before it starts?"

"What if you're fucking wrong? You're talking about driving children, innocents, insane? Maybe even turning them into killers like some of your other epic failures."

The number of failures mounted, as did the death toll. Andrew, who was supposed to be a success, now showed signs of the madness, as did Wes's uncle. One had only to see the feral light in his eyes to recognize it.

"I have allowed you somewhat of a loose rein because you're family." The distaste in Parker's words shone through. "But need I remind you that insubordination will have consequences? I might be fond of Sue-Ellen, but I won't hesitate to wring her neck if you do anything to stand in the way of progress."

And there it was, the implicit threat to someone he loved more than himself. Much as it galled him, Wes couldn't help but plead. "Don't do this. Not to kids."

"Too late. The trials begin tomorrow. Andrew has graciously volunteered his progeny. And soon Fang will be on the hunt for more. We'll even be working on the women in our custody, impregnating them via test tube and, in some cases, by more natural methods. Interested in being a *part of that group, nephew? I hear you have eyes for the woman I brought in."*

The horror of his uncle's offer couldn't stop the hot rage. He hit his uncle! Crack. *A blow that should have knocked the old man on his ass.*

Rubbing his surely-made-of-granite jaw, Parker laughed. "*You'll have to do better than that, nephew.*"

But it wasn't the realization that the modifications had made his uncle so strong that chilled him through and through. It was the peek of familiar eyes from behind a door.

A glimpse seen for a moment then gone.

She's here.

His sister was here. Within reach. At last.

Problem was how to get her out, along with Melanie and her boys.

What of the others also trapped here?

What of them? He cared nothing for the humans who came to work for Bittech. As to those inside the lower levels, those already tainted? Could he truly release monsters onto the world?

"Unleash the beasts!" Melanie's cheerful decree brought his head up. He noted her exiting the building, Rory and Tatum racing ahead of her, their excited squeals filling the quiet morning air.

He knew he saw him standing there. She had to, yet her gaze went right over him. Not welcoming, hell, not even acknowledging. Someone seemed determined to ignore him this morning.

Not today. Wes pushed away from the tree and strode toward her.

90

"Going somewhere, angel?"

"You know, I've only been here a day and I'm already getting tired of hearing that question every time I leave a room."

"You said it best. This is a prison."

"All prisons have a weakness."

Given the missing cameras had yet to be replaced, he didn't have to temper his words. "I'm looking for one."

"I hear a but."

"Because it's going to be tough. This place is nothing like the original Bittech. There is security everywhere. No one goes in or out without authorization."

"What about over the wall?"

"Electrified and eight feet with barbed wire at the top. So unless you're planning to look like that cat in that Chevy Chase Christmas movie, then don't even think of it."

Her lips pursed. Was it wrong to want to kiss them to soften them up? She'd probably slap him if he tried. Then Andrew would have him killed. *Fuck.*

Do it anyway.

His gator loved to live dangerously.

Melanie frowned. "Electrified? Shoot. I'll have to warn the boys not to touch."

"Speaking of your boys, I'm surprised the staff let you out with them."

A smirk tilted her lips. "I didn't give that nurse a choice. I told her they needed fresh air and a run or she'd never get them to cooperate for the tests they plan later."

"You're going to let them touch your kids?" He couldn't help a note of surprise in his tone.

A sly grin tugged at half her lip. "Like hell they are. You told me they only want healthy specimens, right?"

"Yeah."

Still wearing a smile, Melanie walked past the buildings to a part of the compound that, while mown, retained plenty of trees and foliage. A spot of nature amidst supposed progress.

Whooping, the boys ran into the sparse copse, their little bodies bolting and zipping among the trunks.

At the edge, Melanie flopped onto the grass and crossed her legs lotus style.

Her casual pose drew a frown from Wes. "What are you planning?"

Wide eyes with an innocently spoken, "Nothing," did not settle his unease.

Mischief brewed behind her guileless expression. He turned his attention to the boys, cute little buggers with their mother's tanned skin and dark hair. Yet their eyes, those looked nothing like Melanie's—or Andrew's for that matter. The twins seemed healthy and fit. Energetic, too. They played a game of tag, in and out of the trunks, not caring if they caught each other quick or slow. Their laughter rang out as if they didn't have a care in the world.

It left a bitter taste in his mouth as he wondered how much they would laugh once the testing began.

There has to be a way to stop it from happening. He just couldn't see it. Yet. *Because I won't stop until I find a way out for them.*

And I keep telling you it's time to crunch some bones.

Crunching bones won't get us past those gates.

Melanie plucked at the grass, gaze aimed downward as she addressed him. "Why are you following me anyhow? Doesn't Andrew need you to do his bidding? I thought evil overlords liked to keep their henchmen close."

"This is his bidding. Apparently the nurse called him, freaking out about your decision to take the kids outside. He sent me along to keep an eye on you." Of course that had taken a little nudging of Andrew's paranoia.

"You need to keep them safe, or you'll appear weak," Wes warned Andrew.

"Guard them with your life!"

Melanie snorted. "Stuck babysitting me and my boys. How emasculating."

"Thanks for pointing that out," was his wry reply.

"Yeah, especially since you suck at it. You're going to be in a touch of trouble."

"Why?" His gaze immediately went to the boys, who returned with red-smeared lips, the remains of some wild cherries still clutched in their hands.

But more worrisome were the spots all over their skin.

"Guess I'm not getting the mother of the year award because I don't know how I missed spotting the fact you had cherries out here. My boys are highly allergic to them. They get head-to-toe hives and a serious case of the runs."

How awful and yet great because this meant that, until the allergen flushed from their system, no testing could be done.

He couldn't help but laugh because he doubted those

boys had eaten those cherries by accident. Their smell permeated the air, which meant Melanie did it on purpose. "Angel, you're a fucking genius."

Now that she'd given him a little wiggle room to work on an escape plan, he'd better come through because he doubted they'd get a second chance.

Chapter 11

THE GLEE at foiling Andrew's plan to test her boys didn't last. Melanie knew Andrew wouldn't appreciate her not-so-subtle ploy. She also realized an opportunity like that wouldn't happen again. She had only to hear the chainsaws that afternoon and peek out the window to see the cherry trees, actually every tree in the place, taken down.

This meant she had less than a day before the plan to mess with her boys was back on track, and she was no closer to finding an escape.

As evening rolled around, and as she tucked her spotted boys into their beds, she felt Wes's presence. Funny how she never needed to see him to know he'd arrived. For some reason, he exuded a vibe that she couldn't help but pick up on.

It's because he's ours.

She wished her cat would stop with that certainty. She wanted nothing to do with him. "Back to playing

guard? I'm surprised, given your failure of this morning."
She taunted him as she exited the bedroom, shutting the
door behind her.

"Yeah, apparently I didn't get any blame since
Andrew didn't know of your boys' allergy to cherries."

No surprise there. She'd counted on Andrew not
remembering. "Crazy thing to happen, especially to a
shifter, huh?" Because most shifters healed rather rapidly
and rarely got sick.

"Very crazy. So how long before they're
well again?"

"Not long enough," she murmured as they strode the
hall in the direction of the elevator.

The night nurse didn't spare them a glance as they
got in the cab. The doors slid shut, and the crushed
camera meant she could drop her shoulders and sigh. "I
don't know how to get out." As Wes had said, security
was just too damned tight.

"I might have a plan, but we're going to need some
outside help."

Her gaze rose sharply to meet his. "You can get us out
of here?"

"Maybe. But like I said, we're going to need someone
on the outside to pick you and the boys up. I know you
said you didn't want to call anyone, but the plan won't
work without a bit of help."

"How dangerous is it?"

He shot her a look. "Stupid question. So I won't give
you a stupid answer. Anyone you call is going to be in
danger. They might end up killed. Or they might not. It
all depends on how quietly they can sneak. We need

them to get close enough to provide transportation once I get you and the kids out of the compound."

The gears in her mind whirred furiously. She knew Daryl would do it in a heartbeat. No question asked. Hell, Caleb and Constantine would, too. They weren't guys to let a thing like danger get in their way of helping.

The thing was, what if this plan failed? Or what if Wes lied to her and this was simply a ploy to draw those she trusted close so he could nab them for Andrew?

It's a risk I have to take. Because he offered her the only chance she had right now.

"Get me a phone and give me a time and place for Daryl to meet us."

"A phone won't do you any good. They're jammed from receiving or making outside calls."

"So how the hell are you planning to contact him?"

"He's going to get a phone call. It just won't be from me or you. I think I know someone who can get through the fence and call for us."

"How do you know you can trust that person?"

"It's my brother, Brandon."

Exiting from the building, she went silent, as did he, the outdoor cameras having been replaced sometime that day making any conversation they had public knowledge.

If Wes spoke the truth, then he had a plan, and in order for it to work, she had to lull Andrew into thinking she was resigned to her fate.

Speaking of Andrew, "Why does he want to see me?"

After the previous night, she'd thought they were done talking. What could she say to the man who boasted he'd fertilized her with the sperm of another man?

"I don't know what he wants. But I will say, watch yourself. He's not been himself today." Wes whispered those words as they went through the next checkpoint into C building.

The elevator ride, even though there was no camera, happened in silence. What could she say to Wes? *I wish I'd been smarter in my choice of guys. I wish that maybe I'd tried harder when you pushed me away. Hey, your ass looks mighty fine in those jeans tonight.*

Because hitting on the guy escorting her to her husband was such a fine plan.

At the door to Andrew's loft, Wes paused. His eyes were a storm cloud of emotions; she could read so many of them. Worry. Anger. But not at her. Toward her, she sensed frustration and perhaps even a hint of something warmer.

Taking a deep breath that he released in a loud sigh, Wes knocked on the door without saying a word.

Bzzzt. The electronic lock disengaged, and Wes opened the door. He went in first, not because he lacked manners, but because the predator in him must have sensed something amiss and wanted to scout first.

She understood his unease. Within her own mind, her feline prowled. Hackles raised. A low snarl filled her head as the negative vibe within the apartment touched her.

Just ahead of her, she could see Wes tensing. He sensed it, too, a pervasive sour smell of evil. And it came from Andrew.

If she'd thought he looked off kilter yesterday, then Andrew appeared ten times worse today.

Wearing only a loosely belted robe, her *husband*—said with a mental sneer—sat in a club chair, hair in disarray, legs slightly spread, almost enough to expose him.

The by now familiar wild glint in his eye went well with his curled lip.

"If it isn't my dear wife."

"What do you want from me?"

A brow arched. "I'd say that was obvious. A wife's place is by her husband. Serving him."

"I was taking care of my sons."

"You should be taking care of me!" Andrew sprang from the chair, every inch of him vibrating with repressed irritation. "I have needs, too, wife. Needs you've been neglecting for years."

His accusation riled. "Are you seriously going to blame me for the fact you were always too tired or too busy?"

"Maybe it's because you are just too boring."

"Enough," Wes said. He interjected himself between them, and for a moment, she slumped behind his broad back, thankful for the reprieve. Sticks and stones might break bones, but names and accusations cut more deeply.

I told you to stay away from him, her cat chided.

No one likes a smart-ass cat, she snapped back.

"This is none of your affair, gator. Leave." Andrew addressed his icy request at Wes.

"I am not leaving unless I know you won't hurt her."

"What I do with my wife is none of your business."

"You won't be doing anything," she muttered. Playing nice was one thing, allowing this travesty of a man to touch her another.

Andrew heard her denial. "I will do whatever I want to you. And none will dare to stop me."

"I will." Quietly spoken by Wes, yet the words hung quite clearly in the air.

Andrew didn't like them one bit. "What's this? Are you expressing an interest in my wife? Are you the reason she won't fuck me, her husband? If I'd known you were into slumming, dear Melanie, I wouldn't have been so nice."

Crack. The sound of a fist striking flesh brought her around Wes's body. Andrew sat on the ground, rubbing his jaw, but the maniacal smile remained.

"Not bad. And further proof of my so-called wife's perfidy."

"I never cheated on you," she declared hotly.

"And yet your sons are not mine."

"What's he talking about?" Wes growled.

"He's talking about the fact he impregnated me with someone else's sperm. Apparently, I was nothing more to him than an incubator so he could make babies to play god with."

A high-pitched laugh stuttered from Andrew. "I am doing more than playing. I. Am. God."

"No, you're insane. And I want nothing to do with you. I might not be able to escape this place"—*yet*—"but that doesn't mean I can't say no. So unless you're prepared to rape or kill me, I'm leaving," she announced.

"Go. Don't come back unless you're ready to crawl and beg for my forgiveness. But don't be surprised if, when you do, you have to share my bed. A man has needs."

"I won't be back."

"You say that now, but let me add that, if you're not going to be my wife in every way that counts, then you will serve the needs of the project. That is, your womb will. And maybe this time we won't use artificial insemination to get what I need."

Turning on her heel, she tugged blindly at the door, her throat tight and dry. Fear made her hands shake. Wes's smooth grip overtop hers lent some of his strength.

She fled the lair of the madman with only one thought—escape.

Run. Hide. Her cat, usually the bravest of predators, did not know how to handle this level of crazy.

Actually, that was untrue. Her feline did have a solution. A permanent one.

Andrew has to die.

Chapter 12

ENTERING THE ELEVATOR, Wes could sense her turmoil. Hell, he dealt with a whirlwind of it himself.

It took everything in him to not rip into Andrew.

Why do you let him live? He is just meat.

Because dead meat couldn't help him to escape. He needed to find a way to use his proximity to Andrew to execute an escape.

First, though, he had to calm Melanie, even though he felt nothing but stormy himself. He understood, however, she couldn't go back to her boys in this frazzled state.

He stopped the elevator one floor below and dragged her down the hall.

"Where are we going?"

"You'll see," was his reply as he tugged her through the door at the end of the hall and up the stairs. They spilled out onto the roof.

Melanie took a few steps then suddenly dropped to

her knees and screamed. And screamed a little more. Her vocalization came with some choice swear words.

There was nothing gentle about her rage and fear. In that moment, she was a fierce mother, an angry wife. A scared woman.

Comfort her.

He didn't have that right. And he didn't think she would accept it. Not now. Not from him.

When the last echo of emotion faded, her shoulders slumped and her head bowed. Only then did he approach, wary in case she lashed out. She didn't move. He leaned over and grabbed her hand. He drew her to her feet and led her to the far side of the rooftop, away from electronic eyes.

Wait, those eyes were gone. He noted the ragged ends of the wires hanging out. More evidence of vandalism to the cameras. It seemed not everyone enjoyed being under Bittech's watchful gaze.

Wes dropped onto the bench and dragged Melanie onto his lap.

At first she struggled. "Let me go. Don't touch me."

Fuck that. He was done doing what he thought was the right thing for her. Done fighting the fact that he still cared too damned much about Melanie.

He wrapped his arms tightly around her, hugged her like he'd wanted to hug her for years. But he didn't completely lose his balls because he growled, "Calm the fuck down, angel," instead of kissing her.

Should have kissed her. More fun. His gator sulked.

"I won't calm the fuck down," she snarled, glaring at

him with eyes that gleamed wildly. "Andrew's out of his fucking mind."

"Yeah." He couldn't disagree with that assessment.

"My choice is sleep with him or be raped by whomever he chooses."

Like fuck. "Not happening." He'd let his gator go on a rampage first.

"And how are you going to stop it?"

He shrugged. "I'm a Mercer. I'll find a way."

She laughed, a hysterical giggle that turned to wordless high-pitched noises. "I don't know what to do."

"Then do nothing. I'll take care of this."

"How and why? Why put yourself in danger?"

"Because."

"What of your sister? I thought she was the reason you turned to evil."

Wes sighed. "I love my sister. Don't get me wrong. But I can't let you and your boys come to harm." Because, if he did, something inside him would probably die.

"I'm scared, Wes." The softly spoken admission hurt him.

How could words make him ache so badly? *It's because I love her so fucking much still.* The thought of her coming to harm...

"I've got you, angel. I will not let anything happen to you." He palmed her cheeks, forcing her to meet his gaze. "I'd die first." He sealed his promise with a kiss, the salt of her tears flavoring it with bittersweet despair.

At first she remained still under his soft caress, but then, as if a dam within her burst, she came alive in his arms. Her lips pressed insistently against his. Her body turned and leaned into him, the plushness of her ass squirming against the hardness of his cock.

Fucking jeans confined him, but he wouldn't complain, not one word, not when with a simple embrace she ignited all his senses.

I'm on fire. On fire like he hadn't been since they'd broken up. He'd been with women since Melanie, more than his fair share, in an attempt to forget her. None, not a single goddamn one, ever made him feel like she did.

She's mine.

Her mouth parted at the insistent tease of his tongue. He truly got to taste her again, a sensuous slide of flesh, a nibble on her tongue.

His mouth wasn't the only thing busy. His hands roamed her shape, a little fuller than it used to be, a woman's shape, all curves and sexy plushness.

Rearranging her so she straddled him took only a little maneuvering. Melanie seemed as eager as him to get closer. With her facing him, the core of her sex rubbed fully onto his erect shaft.

It didn't matter that clothing separated them. They burned as if they were skin to skin.

Thinking of skin, he slid his hands under the hem of her shirt, stroking the smoothness of her back. His mouth left her swollen lips and nipped along her neck, sucking at her exposed column, her trust in him in that moment absolute.

He kissed the fluttery pulse at the base of her neck. Then went lower. His hands pushed the fabric of her shirt up, up and over the swell of her breasts, the peaks protruding with excitement through the cotton of her bra.

He dipped his head and caught a tip, sucking on it, even though fabric barred his way. She let out a breathy moan. He took more of her breast in his mouth, loving the fullness of it.

Since she had her fingers dug into the muscles of his shoulders, he allowed both his hands to cup and squeeze her ripe peaches. He buried his face between them, inhaling her scent.

Melanie squirmed against him, the heat of her core scorching. He needed to touch it. To touch her. To feel her moistness on his fingers.

Her molding athletic pants did not impede his exploration, but her position did.

"Turn around," he asked.

She quickly complied, turning so she still sat on his lap, facing outward. Leaning back against him, her head rested on his shoulder. He nuzzled her neck as he let his hand skim past the waistband of her pants. He encountered the edge of her panties and slid under those, too.

He cupped her and hissed at her scalding heat. Her sex practically pulsed against him. It certainly wet him with her honey.

With the tip of his fingers, he found her nub and rubbed it. She cried out. He rubbed again then froze as a sound drew his attention.

"Shhh," he whispered in her ear as someone came out on the roof deck.

He kept an eye on them as he continued to circle her clit. They didn't seem inclined to move far from the door, and he could hear the two men—intruders!—chatting in low murmurs as they smoked.

Another time, he might have rebuked them for not using the designated section, but given he pleasured Melanie, he decided to let it pass.

When she squirmed as if meaning to get off his lap, he wrapped his free arm around her and whispered against her ear. "You're not going anywhere. I'm not done."

And by done, he meant with her. For too long he'd tortured himself with the memories of what they shared. Too many nights, as he stroked himself, he recalled her fiery passion, the sweet scent of her honey when she moaned at his touch.

He pinched her button, and she trembled as she whimpered. He murmured, "Remember to keep quiet, angel. We don't want to be discovered."

At his words, she shivered again. She always did so enjoy making love with a fear of discovery. It seemed that hadn't changed.

She relaxed against him and spread her legs wide so they draped on either side of his lap. She gave him complete access to her.

Sweet fucking glory.

Some men were selfish lovers, caring only about giving the woman enough pleasure in order to ensure they got a piece of action.

Not Wes, and never with Melanie. With her, he loved watching her as he stroked her. Loved the hot slickness of her pussy when he slid a finger between her soft folds. Nothing was more beautiful than Melanie with her eyes closed and her mouth parted as he inserted a finger into her tight channel.

He finger fucked her, adding a second and a third digit to his penetration. Her sex clung tight to him, the flesh hot and welcoming. Still so beautifully tight.

Her breath came in short pants as he stroked her faster and faster, the pad of his thumb rubbing against her pleasure button at the same time.

He whispered against her ear. "Come for me, angel. Come for me. Quietly. Now."

She uttered a tiny sob as she obeyed, the muscles of her sex suddenly spasming and undulating as her orgasm crashed through her.

He held her as bliss made her tremble, turned her head and kissed her to catch any sound she might make.

In that moment, he made her his again.

Yes, mine.

And, this time, he wasn't ever going to let her go.

Chapter 13

A PART of Melanie didn't want to leave the rooftop with its panoramic view of the stars. But it wasn't the view that gave her the biggest reason to stay.

Wes did.

Don't I mean Wes did me?

She, a married woman, had let another man touch her. More than touch her, he'd made her *feel*. Feel a sense of closeness and desirability she'd forgotten existed. He'd made her come. Hard. And, dammit, she'd loved it. Loved that sense of feeling alive again.

It was selfish. Wrong. Totally not what she should be doing or thinking, but she didn't regret it. *I refuse to regret it.* She'd spent too many years living as a shell of herself, trying to be someone she wasn't.

I am not a cookie-cutter trophy wife. She'd hated that life. The only good thing that had come out of it was her boys, and it turned out they didn't even belong to Andrew. Given his lies, his actions, and, she realized, her general dislike of the man, as far as she was concerned, she no longer belonged to him either.

Time to move on.

To those who might condemn her actions because she didn't wait for a divorce? To them she raised a middle finger. The marriage had ended the day Andrew inseminated her with someone else's sperm.

And he'd been a dead man living on borrowed time as far as she was concerned the moment he threatened her sons.

"I can hear the gears in your head churning," he muttered against her ear, the hotness of his breath against her lobe.

Since she didn't want to talk about their current situation, she asked him something she'd never really understood. "Why did you really dump me?"

A heavy sigh.

"Wes?"

"You that determined to hash this out now?"

"Yes."

"How about if we just left it at I was an asshole who thought he was doing the right thing."

She tilted her head back to look at him. "How was dumping me, after eating my cake, the right thing?"

"Well, because eating the cake after would have just been a total dick move."

She elbowed him, and yet he still laughed. "This isn't funny," she grumbled. "You broke my heart. And, now, here you are, acting as if you care, and I'm confused."

"It's not an act. I never stopped caring. I cared too

much, which was why I had to let you go. You deserved better than a swamp gator like me with a reputation."

"You thought you weren't good enough for me?" She couldn't help a note of incredulity.

"Look at you. You're gorgeous. Smart. With me out of the way, you could marry a guy with a good name. No family baggage. You could have the life you deserved."

"Are you saying I deserved this?"

"Fuck. No. Of course not."

"Let me explain something to you, Wes Mercer. I settled for Andrew. Settled for a man that did not ignite me with a single look. I settled for a guy who thought work was more important than family. I settled because I couldn't have you."

The words spilled out of her, shocking in their honesty. Spoken, she couldn't take them back. She waited for his reply.

"I can't turn back time."

"What of the future?"

"Until I get you out of here, there is no future."

Bleak outlook, and one she couldn't talk about because more people decided to emerge onto the roof deck, their steps taking them to the shadowy gazebo.

Wes didn't spare them a greeting or glance as he led her from their rooftop bower to the stairs. Only when they were alone in the elevator, free from nosy ears, did Wes mutter, "I'm getting you and the boys out tonight."

"How?"

"I have an idea, so be ready." He yanked her to him for one brief kiss before the elevator shuddered to a stop. "I will come for you."

Would he really?

She wanted to trust in him, especially after his revelation. Wanted to believe him when he said he cared.

But he'd hurt her once before...

Anticipation rendered sleep impossible. As she lay in that barrack room, listening to the soft sounds of her sons' snores, she waited, maybe even fantasized a little about the future.

When we get out of here, maybe we'll move away. Start somewhere new and fresh for both of us. It would be good not only for Wes to escape the Mercer taint, but also for her boys. The quicker they forgot their life with Andrew, the better.

It was time to let go of the mistakes they'd made and forge a new future. A future together.

Because Wes will come for me. The more times she repeated it, the more times she recalled his tender caress, the more she believed it.

In the wee hours of the morning, when the door whooshed opened, it didn't surprise her. Already awake, she sat up, ready to act.

Only the man standing in the doorway wasn't Wes. She could only gape in stunned disbelief at Andrew, especially since he held a gun in her direction.

Uh-oh.

Chapter 14

LEAVING Melanie took everything he had. A part of him wanted to grab her and run. Run fast and far. Now. While they had a chance.

Utter stupidity. Such a rash act would only get them killed or worse. He had to remain calm and steady. No acting until he knew he had a chance of success.

But you promised her an escape tonight.

How could he not when she so desperately needed hope? Thing was, he couldn't afford to make a mistake, just like he couldn't afford to wait any longer.

He had to get Melanie out of here. The sooner, the better. And only one person could help him do that.

He located Brandon perched atop the rooftop of the building their uncle inhabited. A dark gargoyle that could at any moment spread his wings and fly, but who, like Wes, remained chained.

Time to throw off the shackles.

Chances were his brother heard his approach, but

just in case, Wes paused and lit a cigarette. The acrid smell of smoke and the click of his lighter provided enough of an announcement to not startle the predator his brother had become.

Let's not die now.

Don't mistake him. He loved his brother, but at the same time, Brandon was a gator, just like Wes, just like most of the Mercers. Their cold blood ran fierce when it came to keeping the family lines strong. But Brandon was more than that gator now, too. Something darker lived inside him, an entity that wanted to swallow his brother whole. This dark presence kept Brandon from resuming his human shape. Made him a monster, one determined to pick a fight.

"You need a shower," his brother observed. "Or are you intentionally trying to poke the bear by sleeping with his wife?"

"Maybe it's time someone did some poking. I'm tired of being Andrew's fucking patsy."

His brother peered at him over his shoulder. "Was the pussy so good that it completely devalued the life of our sister?"

"No. Of course not. I love Sue-Ellen. You know that. But I also fucking love Melanie. I never bloody stopped. And if I don't do something to help her, Andrew's going to end up hurting her."

"So you slept with her?"

"Not quite. And not the point. Even if I wasn't in love with her, I couldn't stand by and do nothing when I know Andrew's planning to hurt those boys."

"Ah yes. The children. They have such an interesting

smell about them," Brandon whispered, turning his head away to again face the darkness.

It chilled Wes's blood to hear his brother speak that way. "When did you get a chance to sniff them?"

"Parker has had me playing bodyguard as he wanders around the compound. It seems our venerable uncle doesn't trust his new lackeys."

"Afraid his monsters might rip his throat out?" Wes surely found himself tempted.

"He should be afraid. If not for Sue-Ellen, he'd be dead already."

"She's here, you know."

His brother whirled from the parapet. "What?"

"I said she's here. I saw her, in Parker's apartment."

"I smelled nothing."

It surprised Wes to realize he didn't recall scenting her either. That stupid cologne. It took from shifters one of their main advantages. "I'm telling you I saw her."

"We must help her escape. Once she's gone..."

"Then the ties binding us are, too," Wes finished. "We also have to take Melanie and the twins."

"You ask much, brother. It will be hard enough for us three to slip the leash, but to add in others? We will be caught."

"I won't leave without her. I have a plan."

"Does it involve three magical wishes?" his brother retorted.

"No, but it does require one flying lizard."

Brandon hunched farther. "Then it's doomed to fail."

"What are you talking about?"

"I am going to assume you mean to have me transport everyone over the fence."

"Yes. Once we're out, we'll start running, and you can fly ahead and call someone for help."

"Except we can't get to the other side of the fence." Brandon hopped off the ledge and turned to face him. His fingers hooked under the collar circling his neck. The collar that controlled his actions. "There have been some new modifications to the collar. Starting with tracking devices in all of them and a trigger when we get within ten feet of the fence."

"So fly twenty feet over."

Brandon shook his head. "Lester tried that. Let's just say roasted psycho lizard smells like chicken when it hits a fence and fries. Whatever signal Bittech is emitting extends into the air. I'm just as penned as you are, landlubber."

"Well, that fucking blows my plan to shit."

"It's hopeless," Brandon said with a shrug of his shoulders. "Perhaps it's time we accepted it."

Accept being a prisoner? Accept the fact that Melanie would hate him and blame him if something happened to her kids?

There had to be a way out of this mess. A way for them all to escape.

Then again, did they all need to escape? What if a single person could slip away? What if they could get word to those in Bitten Point? Surely someone would come to their rescue.

"Follow me, but stay out of sight," Wes advised as he strode across the roof to the access door.

"What the fuck are you planning?"

A quick glance showed the cameras had suffered the same fate here as elsewhere.

"We are going to rescue Sue-Ellen, and then, she's going to rescue us."

"How? I thought you said she was with our uncle."

Wes, with one hand on the door, replied, "I am going to cause a distraction. Once I do, you grab her and fly as fast as you can to that fucking fence and toss her."

"You want me to chuck our sister like a football?"

"Yes."

"And what if she's got a bracelet or collar, too."

"Then we're fucked."

"More than fucked," announced Parker with a shove on the door that sent Wes reeling. "What naughty nephews, planning mutiny."

"Get out of here, Brandon," Wes yelled, lunging at his uncle.

But his brother didn't leave, and Parker hadn't come alone. Riddled with darts, Wes sank to his knees, blinking slowly. Sinking.

He whispered, "Melanie," and then a blow to the head sent him into darkness.

Chapter 15

WHERE IS WES? Melanie failed miserably at hiding her shock upon seeing Andrew in the doorway of the room.

"Expecting someone else, dear wife?"

"What are you doing here?" she asked, the beginning of fear trembling inside. "It's the middle of the night."

"I know, and yet I couldn't sleep. I got some bad news, you see, and since I was awake, I thought why not come over and take you to your new quarters."

"I'm not going anywhere."

Andrew arched a brow. "Really? Funny because the way I heard it, you're not happy with your current situation. Rumor has it you're thinking of running away."

"I don't know what you're talking about," she lied.

"Did you really think I wouldn't find out about your little plan with the gator to escape? He told me everything."

"You're lying."

"Maybe I am. Maybe I'm not. Doesn't really matter. You're still being moved. I have plans for you."

"You can take those plans and stuff them up your tight, repressed ass." Probably not the best idea to antagonize him, but she couldn't sit back and allow him to threaten her.

His eyes narrowed, cold and menacing. "If I were you, I'd really watch that tongue. You don't need it for what I have planned."

Red-hot anger mixed with icy fear wouldn't let her cower. "Touch me and I will kill you."

"Did you know your gator lover threatened the same thing not even an hour ago? I put him in his place."

The words chilled her. "What did you do to Wes?"

"You should be more worried about what I plan to do to you."

"Don't you touch my mama!" Rory yelled before launching himself from the top bunk.

He never hit his target. A rapid blur of movement resulted in a tall lizard dude catching her son mid-flight.

It wasn't Ace. Even more worrisome, there was nothing human in this reptile's gaze. "Smellsss good."

It flicked a tongue and licked her son, and it was only her prior knowledge that the saliva acted as a paralytic that kept her from freaking when Rory went limp. She didn't dare do anything, lest the sharp claws holding Rory puncture baby skin.

Tatum began to wail in his bunk. "You're a meanie!"

With a scowl of annoyance, Andrew barked. "Stop that noise at once."

"Make me!" Tatum launched himself at the man he

thought was his father. Given he was on the lower bed, he had no problem scooting across the floor until he sank his teeth into Andrew's leg.

"You little bastard!" Andrew screamed.

Pussy.

With the distraction, Melanie knew she had to act and prayed that she didn't miscalculate. *They need the boys. The lizard thing won't hurt Rory.* She hoped.

She dove at Andrew, intent on getting her hands on the gun, but she'd not counted on the third person to enter the room.

Parker.

It took only his cold gaze and tersely uttered, "Stop your antics this instance, or both your children will die," for her to freeze in her tracks.

Andrew might not want to kill her babies—he needed them for his perverse plans—but this man... The evil within him didn't care who he harmed.

"Get this thing off me," Andrew snapped, shaking his leg but unable to dislodge Tatum.

Tossing a limp Rory onto the bed, the lizard thing went to his boss's aid and licked her poor son.

Gross, but they'd recover. She on the other hand? She was in a big heap of trouble.

"Do I need to have Fang get a taste of you, too, or are you going to be a good girl and behave?"

Since she needed to survive in order to escape, she bowed her head with a meekness she didn't feel. But she wouldn't promise. She just let her feet shuffle in the direction they pointed, and as she did, she gave a message to her boys. "Don't worry, babies. Why don't you play a game of manhunt while you're waiting for Mama to come back for you?"

"How optimistic of you, dear wife."

She shot Andrew a glare. "Not your wife for long because, first chance I get, I'm making myself a widow."

"Is this where I mention the fact our marriage was never valid?"

She blinked, thrown for a loop at his words. "What are you talking about? Of course we're married. We have the damned thing on video."

"My father managed to have it annulled when the brats were born."

Shoved into the elevator, she whirled and had to ask, "Why?"

"Because that was when my father drew me into his plans. I am destined for greatness. I deserve better than a swamp girl as my wife."

"You're a snob."

"Thank you." Andrew's leer stretched wide.

Parker didn't join them in the elevator, having stopped by the nurses' station on the nursery level to have a word.

Bracketed between Andrew and his lizard hench-man, the elevator dropping levels—...three, two, one, sub level A, B...—she didn't get a chance to run.

Even if I did manage to slip them, where would I go? She still had no way over the fence, and she couldn't leave without her boys.

The elevator finally stopped moving, and the doors slid open. Given she could hear ominous music in her head, she kind of expected to emerge into the bowels of

Hell. Instead, she noted they were in a large control room. Numerous screens hung on the wall, with a pair of human guards watching them.

She couldn't help but scan the images on the screen, images of cages for the most part lining an empty corridor. "What is that?"

"Welcome to our experimental levels. It's where we keep our test subjects as they go through their changes."

Changes? The very thought made her stomach clench. "How many people are you experimenting on?"

"Not as many as we'd like. We had to dispose of a few during the move. But never fear. We'll gather more."

"To do what?"

"Ah, there is that famous curiosity known in cats." Andrew's smile displayed too many teeth. "Do you want to see? Do you truly want to *see*?" he asked, his voice dropping a few octaves. Andrew achieved a darkness in his words and a coldness in his eyes that brought a shudder.

Smart people ran when they recognized the presence of true evil. Melanie angled her chin. She'd married this monster. She should bear the burden of seeing what he'd wrought under her nose. "Show me what you've done."

"With pleasure. Come and bask in the glory that is science." Andrew stepped to the sealed metal portal. "Open the doors."

The doors clanked, and air hissed as they slid open. A veritable bunker meant to keep things in and not get out.

Andrew stepped in. Nudged from behind, and worried about Fang who whispered, "Tasssty," Melanie followed.

The smell of wrongness hit Melanie as she crossed the threshold, and she froze.

I can't go in there. To go in there was to set eyes upon madness. To see her possible future.

She spun, ready to run, but there was nowhere to go. Clawed fingers grasped at her and whirled her forward. The reptilian henchman frog-marched her into Hell.

As soon as she entered, she couldn't help but utter a horrified sob as she saw the true purpose of Bittech.

The first few cages held a few people still seemingly normal. According to her nose, some were actually humans. Was he turning them into monsters, too?

These scared people in cages gripped the bars at their approach, turning pleading eyes toward them. "Help us."

"I will help, and soon. Then all of you will thank me for improving you," Andrew announced with the arrogance of a madman wearing a twisted crown of blood and insanity.

So far, not so bad, but the smell of wrongness lingered, and it didn't emanate from these people. They went farther into this hidden level, a cluster of empty cells giving her a reprieve. Still, nothing could have prepared her for the appearance of the monsters past those.

Their alien stench hit her hard, but not as hard as the frightening hunger in their inhuman gaze.

"You have more of the lizard things," she stupidly noted aloud.

"We refer to them as our hunter models."

"Your what?" Melanie drew her gaze from the raptor-like monstrosities with hooked beaks, whipping tails, and leathery wings, barbed on the tips. Scary Fang, who guided her steps, looked cute and cuddly compared to this bunch.

"You are looking at our aerial soldier models. Swift. Deadly. And—"

"Fucking nuts." She didn't mean Andrew and his pride in this twisted creation, but rather the deadly hunger in those monstrous eyes. "These are killing machines." Killing machines with no humanity left in them. Then again, given their captivity in cages barely big enough to stand in, was it any wonder?

"Killing machines." Andrew chuckled. "Indeed they are and in high demand from certain government factions. Once we fine-tune the command collars, they'll fetch a lovely penny."

"You're selling them?"

"Bittech is selling all kinds of things. Soldiers, upgrades, even the chance for the richer humans to become a shifter themselves, for the right price."

"The world will notice what you're doing. You can't blatantly unleash these things and not get caught. How can you risk all of our kind for money?"

"Perhaps it's time we stopped hiding. Parker says—"

"This is Parker's idea?"

"Parker has a vision. One where, instead of the wolves hiding from the sheep, the wolves rise and take their rightful place."

"The humans won't stand for it. They outnumber us. You'll kill us all if you out us."

"Not if we kill them first. And you will help us with that. We're going to need soldiers. Strong, able-bodied shifters loyal to us, born and raised under a new doctrine."

What a frightening vision. "I won't help you."

"You don't have a choice." Andrew stopped before an empty cell. "Say hello to your new home."

Panic clawed at her, but her inner panther scratched harder.

Run, her feline screamed. *Run before they cage us.*

Her sudden yank saw her slipping the grip of the lizard guard, and she sprinted, ran as quickly as she could, only to have a heavy body slam into her from behind.

It took only a slimy lick for her to slump. But it was the needle jabbed in her arm that dragged her eyelids down.

Chapter 16

"URGH." Wes sucked in a deep breath, similar to that of a man grabbing his first breath after drowning. A needle receded from him, the pinching pull of it sliding out not something a man ever forgot. The shot of adrenaline zinged through his body and yanked his consciousness from a dark abyss, shoving it rudely into bright fluorescent lights. The kind of lights that said, "Oh shit."

Oh shit number two came when Wes realized the restraints holding his wrists and ankles wouldn't budge.

A word of advice if this ever happened to anyone. Waking up to find yourself tied and spread-eagle in an operating theatre never boded well. For anyone! Seriously. It didn't, especially since he seemed to have lost most of his clothes. He wore only his form-fitting boxers. And before a wrong conclusion occurred that cheesy music would begin to play before some debaucheries, keep in mind, again, that real life did not suddenly turn into porn at the loss of his pants. At least by leaving his underpants, they left him a little dignity.

Not little, his gator slyly remarked. *Those puny cowards didn't wish to expose our impressive girth.*

In a gator's world, size did matter in a lot of things.

Turning his head, Wes noted Dr. Philips, whom he recognized from the old Bittech. The doctor, with no scruples, having been ousted by a pharmaceutical firm for unlawful experimentation, used to work in the secret installation. There wasn't a thing this doctor wouldn't do. Science had made him hard. Subjects dying due to failure didn't bother him in the least.

Seeing him made his gator wary, especially since Dr. Philips held a giant fucking needle.

"What the hell are you planning to do with that thing?" Because in no sane world did a needle that size do good things. Ever.

"Do?" Dr. Philips seemed surprised at the question. "Why, my job, of course." Not the most reassuring of words.

Washed-out blue eyes regarded him. It took Wes a moment to realize Dr. Philips no longer wore his glasses. He'd also misplaced his stooped shoulders. The thinning hair atop his head hung in lusher hanks. As a matter of fact, Dr. Philips looked like a taller, prouder, thicker version of himself.

"What the hell did you do to yourself?" Wes asked with a pitch of incredulity. It didn't take a reply, though, to figure it out. What he had to wonder was, what sane man would inject those dangerous cocktails into his own body after having seen firsthand the possible madness and deformities?

Not everyone would care about the risk, not when they saw so much to gain.

He sees the strength he can have.

Vanity. Greed. Want. His gator understood, wanting to be the biggest and baddest. The strongest males controlled. The strongest males survived. But what of when the lowest ones applied unnatural enhancements? Who became the alpha then?

"What have I done?" The doctor smiled. "What everyone will soon be clamoring to do. A new evolution is coming to mankind. We are about to embark on the next step, and as one of the creators, I am one of the first to enjoy the fruits of my labor."

"Are you already out of your fucking mind? Have you forgotten the raving lunatics that have emerged from some of these tests?"

The doctor made a dismissive noise. "Early mistakes that have since been corrected."

The needle still hovered, and Wes hated the trepidation he felt when he asked, "What's in that thing? It better not be one of your goddamned enhancements. I like myself just fine as is."

"As if we'd waste such an elixir on someone like you." Dr. Philips squirted some liquid into the air, the tiny droplets catching the light and Wes's attention. "The fluid in this needle is meant to prep you for the insemination phase."

What the fuck! Wes's mind processed the words. Rejected them. Tried again. Freaked the hell out.

Freaked out even more when he could do nothing to stop the needle from plunging into his thigh. He bucked in his restraints. "What the hell did you just inject me with? What are going to do to me?"

"Let me explain it in words my stupid nephew will understand. Dr. Philips here is going to make sure your swimmers are ready to go because you're going to need them to fuck and impregnate a woman." The cold statement from his uncle saw Wes whipping to peek at the other side of him. The bastard had snuck up on him. How that peeved. But Wes could only blame himself and his cigarette habit.

Bloody smoking dulled his sense of smell. The nicotine clung and prevented him from deeply tasting of the scents.

If I get out of here, make that when, I'm quitting, cold fucking gator.

Seeing Parker's smug smile made Wes forget the restraints that bound him. He lunged, his body arcing off the table, yet for all his straining, he remained pinned.

"You fucking bastard. I'm going to bloody kill you."

Parker angled his head as he tsked. "What a futile threat given you're so helpless I could slit your throat right now and there isn't a damned thing you could do about it."

"Try it." Dying might be preferable to what they planned.

Dying is cowardly.

Fucking honor.

Parker neared and stared down at him. Wes's exposed bare skin pimpled at his perusal.

"Don't tempt me, nephew. I came close once I discovered your plotting. Lucky for you, you have excellent genes."

Snort. "Given they're Mercer genes, I'd beg to disagree," Wes stated.

A hand waved away his words. "You see only the reputation. A reputation that you idiots perpetrate. Move away from here and start fresh. Live the life you choose. The Mercers in Bitten Point are only restricted by themselves. They don't have to live under that stigma."

"Funny, you moved away, and yet you're probably the dirtiest Mercer of all."

"Dirty for wanting better for myself? Is it wrong to want greatness? Power?" His uncle's brows rose. "And this is the problem with the Mercers of Bitten Point. Always thinking small."

"Then why come back? Why use us to further your sick goals?"

"The reason is simple. The Mercer branch of Bitten Point has excellent genes. Healthy genes. Strong ones."

"If it's so strong, then why mess with it?"

"Because it's precisely that strength that we need. When you add some elements from other species, our strong DNA handles it better than most. It's why the Mercers are so valuable to this project. Our blood seems able to handle anything." Parker's eyes shone, but the frightening thing about his fervor? The madness Wes noticed before no longer inhabited his gaze.

He's not insane anymore. He's calm and convinced.

Somehow, that seemed more worrisome.

"Is that why you took Brandon? And now me? To test your cocktail on us?"

"Your brother ended up serving as the answer to why it didn't work. You will help create the next generation that will."

"What the hell are you talking about? I am not helping you do shit."

"Really?" The smile on his uncle's face took his cold blood and turned it to ice. "Then I guess you don't mind if we use someone else to fornicate and impregnate Melanie. Odd, because I would have thought you'd prefer to handle it yourself."

Snap. With a roar not meant for human lips, Wes surged from the bed, parts of him shifting and bulging. A gray deadly haze filtered his gaze while strength coursed through his limbs.

The puny restraints could not withstand his yank. Nothing could cage him. He would kill the thing before him that dared call itself family.

He swiped, and the male dodged his strike and then stopped him with words.

"Harm me and I will give Melanie to the less savory results of our experiments."

Despite the cold thoughts running through his head, Wes retained enough wits to know Parker meant it.

He wants to hurt my angel. He couldn't allow Melanie to come to harm, and yet his need to protect the female he considered his mate warred with his instinct to protect his sister. How to resolve it?

Kill him.

The simplest solution and the only way to ensure the

man couldn't hurt anyone he cared for anymore. But an attempt now would never fly.

We have to bide our time, my cold friend. Do as I ask for now, and when the chance arises, we shall wreak our vengeance.

Crunch some bones? his gator self asked.

Crunch them with glee—after dousing them in hot sauce. His gator did so like things with a little bite.

Let's make him think he's won for now. He needed to glean more of the situation. Wes hung his head, unable to meet his uncle's gaze for fear the smirk of triumph Parker surely sported would make him snap again.

"I'll do as you ask." He almost choked on the words. He no longer wanted to listen. He was done being a pawn for his uncle and Andrew. But he had to be smart about this.

"Obeying won't be the horrible task you're worried about, nephew. You get to fuck your old girlfriend Melanie. You will do your best to impregnate her."

Was it possible to hate and want what Parker offered at the same time?

"I will." Because hopefully she would see his touch as the lesser of so many evils. He hoped. He also hoped to find a chance to escape.

And crunch some bones on the way. Snap.

"Stand still as Dr. Philips gives you the second shot."

More fucking needles. "What's the second one for?"

"It's to ensure you're up to the task. Can't have you limp for the next phase."

"I don't need help."

"Perhaps not, but just to be sure you don't balk, you will let the doctor administer it. Or else."

Again with the threats that made him impotent. What could he do? Nothing but let Dr. Philips approach with his second, smaller syringe. Wes leaned against the medical bed, and stared at his bare feet rather than the doctor. He had to look away because otherwise he might lose his shit completely and kill him. The rage simmered at his surface, an almost living, breathing thing.

A power he would use when the right time hit.

Not yet.

But soon. So soon.

The sharp prick of the needle didn't disturb. It was the thought of what they injected him with that did.

"If this is some kind of aphrodisiac, then what was in the first one you gave me?"

"That mixture was a serum to temporarily enhance your animal side and remove the block we placed on your ability to shift."

"You did what?" He forgot his own promise to not look and shot his uncle a glare.

"We give it to all shifters in our control to ensure compliance and because angry animals are hard on our human staff. You wouldn't believe the money it takes to cover up a death these days."

Give the guy credit. It took balls to complain about the hardship that came with being a murdering sociopath. "When the hell did you give that blocking shit to me? I haven't had any needles or blood work done in a while."

"It's in the food." His uncle grinned. "And you never even noticed."

"It also didn't work so good," Wes taunted right back, "given I managed to half shift a few minutes ago."

That brought a frown to Parker's face. "So I noted. Odd because the serum shouldn't have worked that quickly. The formula might require some adjustment."

Great. Wes and his big mouth had just ensured he'd get drugged harder the next time. "Why are you taking this blocker off anyhow? Aren't you afraid I'll snap and eat some guards?" Wes couldn't help a predatory, toothy grin.

"We've run into an interesting dilemma. Having the beast side repressed affects the sperm ejected during climax. In other words, you shoot. If we want to succeed, then we need your animal genes to fertilize."

"Why not just test tube the babies?" he asked, not because he didn't crave Melanie's body against his but because, to him, it made no sense. "You know interspecies mating is hard. The chances of me getting her pregnant are pretty small."

"Except for the fact her body's been conditioned with fertility treatments to accept implantation. And we've enhanced her eggs within her ovaries as opposed to after we've harvested them. For some reason, very few enhanced in-vitro specimens survive. They lack something in their conception that we think can be solved with true coital procreation."

"Does Melanie know you turned her body into some kind of genetic farm?"

Parker smiled. "Andrew wisely made her think all the

treatments she received were to make her more fertile. Which isn't exactly untrue. It just wasn't making her fertile for his sperm. The man's balls are devoid of life, much like his personality," his uncle confided.

"Why are you telling me all this?"

"Why not? Who are you going to tell? And even if you did find someone to listen, so what? I think it's time the world knows who we are so I can share with them what I am doing."

The claim caught his attention. "What do you mean, the world? You sound as if you're planning to announce what you're doing and what we are."

"Because I am." Parker took on a calculated gaze. "It's time we came out of the shadows, nephew, and took our rightful place. As leaders."

"You can't fucking—"

"Reveal us to the humans? Why not?" Parker's grin said it all.

And Wes suddenly realized it wasn't just him and Melanie and everyone else held prisoner at Bittech that was in trouble, but all of shifter kind.

Fuck. *The Mercer reputation is about to get even worse.*

Chapter 17

SITTING UP ON A CONCRETE FLOOR—WHICH
really lacked the comfort of her pillow top mattress at
home—Melanie tried to not let fear control her first
waking thought. Although she certainly had reason to
shake in her boots, if her feet weren't bare.

Actually, most of her was kind of naked except for the
paper gown covering her, a giant tissue with holes for her
arms and a big gaping seam at the back. She certainly
hadn't dressed herself in it, and the fact that she didn't
remember anything past the point where the lizard thing
had taken her down really freaked her out.

What happened while I was asleep? It didn't take a
vivid imagination to think all kinds of awful things. She
palpated herself, hands running over her limbs looking
for sore spots, anything that might have indicted abuse
or worse.

Stomach a tight knot, she stared at the pinprick hole

in her arm. A needle mark. What had they injected her with?

She didn't feel any different. *Kitty, are you in there?*

Rowr. The discontented rumble of her cat relieved her, but that feeling was short-lived as she tried to shift and couldn't.

Not even a single hair.

Crap. Still blocked.

Meow. A sadder sound she'd never heard.

Don't worry, kitty. I'll find a way to get you out.

Since she couldn't unleash her beast and roar her displeasure, she perused her prison.

Her new bedroom sported the latest in jail cell décor. It featured a concrete wall at the back and bars on the other three sides. "He put me in one of those goddamned cages." She couldn't help but utter her disbelief aloud. Sure, Andrew had said he would, but a part of her truly hadn't believed it. Thought it was a ploy to get her to behave.

Wow, was she ever wrong. Again. She truly needed to stop underestimating this new version of Andrew. He seemed ready to do anything at all.

The entire situation wasn't good. Not good at all. First off, she really preferred comfortable cotton—less chafing on the skin. Second, people wearing paper gowns in cages didn't have a good prognosis. Especially when in the custody of Bittech and the mad men running it.

I don't want to be a monster.

She sat up and peeked around. Still the same set of bars and direness. *I need out of this cage.*

But how? She stood and walked to the bars, peeking through them to the one across from her. Whoever lived in that cage slept, a hump under a wool blanket. But she didn't care about the person in the cage. She peeked at the lock and could have cheered when she noted they'd gone old-style padlock. Thick ones that wouldn't break on a good pull. The kind that needed a key.

Sweet, old-fashioned tumbler lock. Electric panels, while sleek and cool, relied on electricity and ideal conditions. A little too much moisture, or dust, even a surge of power and the components fried.

The last thing they'd want was for a lock to fail and loose a monster.

I wonder if I can open it.

Now, most people knew Melanie as the respectable wife of Andrew Killinger. She kept a nice home—in between the boys destroying it. She cooked lovely meals —often with a bit of spice because it was the only way her husband ever sweated. She also had a sex toy party—done to shock the ladies at the institute, only to end up shocked herself since most of them owned the implements of pussy torture already.

Sad to realize she was the prude of the group.

However, all that stuff wasn't really who Melanie was. Melanie had grown up on the same wrong side of the tracks as the Mercers of Bitten Point. Her family was just smaller and nicer to people.

Yet, being nice didn't mean she didn't have her share of vices. One of her interests in her teens ran to lock picking. It obsessed her. The idea people could hide secrets or, in her mother's case, the junk food that would rot her teeth.

Lithe fingers made for nimble fingers. And nails, especially long feline ones, could do more than scratch. Lock picking became an art.

But to make it work, I need to grow kitty nails. She'd just tried and had not been able to pull on her cat at all.

Try again.

She couldn't worry if she didn't even attempt.

Closing her eyes, she took a deep breath.

Here kitty, kitty.

Really? She could practically see the disdain in her feline's tilted head.

Wanna play with a lock? Because once they got out of this cage, her cat would probably have a lot of playtime. *Hope you're in the mood to spar and run.*

Always. Her cat practically purred in her head.

Okay, here goes nothing. She imagined her claw growing from the tip of her index finger.

Given her last failure, she almost expected it to not work. But she could have cried when the sharp tip pulled at her existing nail, reshaping into something long and more needle-like. She did it to the index finger on her other hand. Then she hugged her cage.

Her slim arms slid between the bars with ease. For a moment, she feared cameras watched. *They'll know what I'm doing.*

Then I'd better move quicker.

Face smooshed against the bars to give herself the most wiggle room with her arms, she went to work, poking at the lock, wishing she wasn't years out of practice.

A click sounded, a mechanical indicator a door had opened. Since playing opossum could provide valuable clues, she flattened herself on the floor, shutting her eyes, and feigning sleep.

Footsteps approached, and she heard the murmurs of two men talking in a low tone.

"Have you finished the preliminary workup on female patient PK1?"

"Yes. Her blood work matches that previously on file. Another dose of DRG4.1C was administered."

"She showed no adverse signs?"

"None."

"What of the two subjects being held in the nursery unit?"

Melanie bit her fist as she strove to not scream the question burning the tip of her tongue—*are they talking about my boys?*

"The initial blood work and measurements have been taken. The results are good. Some time later today or tomorrow, we will begin dosing subjects PK2 and PK3."

"Why later?"

The other man did not reply.

A huff of impatience filled the silence. "I said why later? Mr. Parker will want to know why there is yet another delay in getting that part of the project moving."

A heavy sigh was followed by a scuff of fidgeting feet. "The subjects seem to have disappeared."

"What do you mean disappeared?"

"Exactly that. The nurse on duty left them secured in the specially designed playroom. When she returned, they were gone."

"Gone? How the hell did they manage to lose both boys?"

If Melanie wondered before, she knew now. *They're talking about Rory and Tatum.* By the sounds of it, her boys had managed to hide themselves.

She wished she could fist pump in glee. Maybe they'd managed a way to escape or at least hide until the cavalry arrived, which should be any day, any hour, any second now. It was, after all, the plan, the one she'd concocted when she encased the second little GPS tracker in bubblegum and swallowed it before going on her road trip with Parker. She had to hope Daryl noted it was gone. There had been no time that night to leave a note, and she hadn't dared say anything aloud in case Andrew or his goons listened. Hell, she'd not even thought about the damned device making its way through her digestive tract since her capture. With the monsters Andrew created, who knew what he was capable of. What if flying wasn't the only ability he cultivated? What if he'd found a way to read minds?

Then he'd know how much I hated him.

Although, deciphering that didn't need a mind reader. She declared her dislike every time she spoke to or about Andrew.

Back to the tracking device. Daryl would have noticed it was gone and made the connection, which meant he would have been following her. She hoped. She wasn't too sure if the signal still worked once she ingested it.

If she miscalculated, then she was in a heap more trouble than expected. She'd not expected, once she got within the new Bittech complex, that she wouldn't get a chance to get in touch with anyone on the outside.

Everything rests on Daryl now.

What of Wes? Given Andrew's claim, she could only hope he still lived.

The guy outside her cell didn't sound too happy as he said, "I want those brats found. Stupid rotten felines. I hate working with them. Such sly, disgusting creatures."

Going to slyly rip your face off. Rowr.

Her cat took insults very personally.

"When are we beginning the next phase with the female?"

"She has already been added to the implantation roster. They want her starting as soon as possible."

"I thought the other feline subject was pregnant."

"There are complications."

It took all her self-control not to shudder at the reminder of the heap of fur with misshapen limbs, distended belly, and expressive eyes that had begged for death.

And now this psycho wanted to do the same to her!

"Which in-vitro treatment is she receiving?"

"No in-vitro for her. Misters Parker and Killinger are both insisting she be slated for actual implantation by another subject."

"Who's the lucky guy who gets a piece of her tail?"

"Whoever the boss says. Makes me kind of wish we were taking the mods. It could be us."

Did either of them see the shudder that shook her body?

"Get her room prepped. Once we're done here, I'll find out from the bosses who they want to use with her."

"I'll put her in implantation room number two. It's got viewing windows."

"Excellent plan. Do you have the needle ready? We need to get her injected with the serum to remove the block before she's transported."

"Locked and loaded."

The jangle of keys and the scrape of one against metal let her know they planned to get in the cage with her.

It took every ounce of will she possessed to keep still. All she wanted to do was jump to her feet and pound on the bars while elucidating the things she'd do to the pair of them when she got loose. They proved colorful and, in one instance, involved a certain hot spice shoved where no light shone.

The imaginative ways she thought of to hurt the men kept her from moving long enough that they opened the cage and came right in.

That's it. Get closer. Come here, you bastards, so I can give you a nice scratch.

She could feel them staring at her.

"She's a hot one. I still can't believe the boss put her down here. I thought they were married."

"It's not our place to speculate. Inject her."

"Are you sure she's sleeping?" he asked with a little trepidation.

"She should be for at least another hour. She's not one of the enhanced subjects, so the drugs still work well on her."

No, they didn't, but she wasn't about to correct them. Nor was she keen to let them stab her with the needle. But without her cat, could she really take on two men?

Jab.

The inner musings took too long. The plunger came down, and with a scream, she reared up.

In the second it took her to open her eyes, really open her eyes, she noted things with a crystal clarity that only seemed to come in times of great turmoil.

For one, the pair of guys in the cage with her were human. Puny. Scared. Humans.

And whatever was in that needle didn't put her to sleep, or hurt.

On the contrary, it ignited her senses, especially those of her hunter side. She rolled to her hands and knees, belly low, lip curled in a snarl. While she might still wear her human shape, they had enough sense to feel the menace radiating off her.

The older of the two guys went scrambling for the open cage door while the other pressed against the back. She went for the one trying to take away her freedom.

She tackled him, her lithe body springing and hitting his with enough force to send him falling to the floor. His head snapped back and hit the concrete, and his eyes shut as he went limp. And she made sure he stayed that way —permanently.

In the bayou, there was only one law when it came to surviving—kill or be killed.

One down. A blubbering one to go. She turned around, a short Latina in a blue paper gown, and yet, the other man shivered in the cell, his eyes wide.

"Don't hurt me."

She took a step toward him and was pleased when her fingers managed to pop claws.

"OHGODNO!"

He begged. He screamed. She showed him no mercy. She couldn't. He wouldn't have shown her any, and judging by what she'd seen, the pleas of all the prisoners went unheeded.

Suffer not the guilty. He paid for his crimes, noisily, and yet no one came running to his aid.

Once he died, silence fell in the massive containment level. The other cages around her were quiet, except for the occasional whimper. The despair in the air tried to cling. How long had it taken to break these people? She didn't intend to stay and find out.

She exited the cage and stooped to grab the keys the first man had in his possession.

"What are you doing?" a voice whispered.

"Getting out of here," she replied as she tugged the ID bracelet off the guy, too. It probably wouldn't work for her, but it didn't hurt to have.

"Those who try to escape are always punished."

Melanie let her gaze rove until she located the speaker two cells to her left. The young, rotund man clutched at his bars.

"They'll also punish me if I stay. I'll take my chances. You can escape, too." She shook the keys at him.

"No thanks. I'm not going to get punished. I like it here."

Like it? She couldn't help but gape at him. "Are you insane? How can you like it? They're planning to inject you with drugs to change you."

The man shrugged. "At first, I was kind of pissed, but the shots they give us aren't so bad. They're better sometimes than the drugs I used to take."

She narrowed her gaze at the guy. "They've been experimenting on you?"

"Yes." He sounded so happy, and she noted the shine of madness in his eyes. "The one they just tried on me almost lets me turn into a bear. At least my arms and legs."

"What were you before?"

"A nobody. I didn't even know people could change into animals before coming here."

She'd stepped closer as she spoke to him, close enough to smell his twisted essence. "You're human."

"Not anymore," he said with glee. "And neither will you be. If you survive, they might even let me have you. The next stage of the program is to see if we can cross breed." He leered between the bars. "I can't wait to start."

Not with her he wasn't. Any thought she'd had to let him out evaporated. Right now, she had to ensure her own escape, which meant getting her chubby ass out of there before she became crazy patient number one hundred and ninety-seven.

Ignoring the guy who now moaned and dry humped

the bars, Melanie walked past his cage toward the other end of the massive containment level.

But the guy didn't let her leave unchallenged.

"What are you doing? Get back in your cage. Guards. Guards, she's escaping."

Melanie couldn't believe the guy was ratting her out. Even worse, the other prisoners began rattling their bars, too, and shouting.

Hell no. She couldn't get caught again. *I have to get out.* She bolted past the cages where people—and things—rose to their feet shouting.

"She's escaping."

"Don't leave me here."

"I feel like chicken tonight."

The variety of suggestions showed the different levels each prisoner had reached. Some were almost hunter ready.

They were scary, almost as scary as the fact that there was only one door out of here that she could see. For some reason, it made her think of the song "Hotel California" by The Eagles. Once checked in, could she escape? She had to. If she got caught, she might never get another chance.

The elevator door didn't yield at her shove. The video screen alongside it stated a simple, "Please tap your access card."

Unfortunately, prisoners didn't get the same perks as the doctors and henchmen did. She wanted to sob at the injustice. What kind of stupid building required special privilege to move floor to floor?

One designed to keep secrets in.

She tried slapping the access bracelet she'd stolen from the dead guy's wrist.

The screen turned red. Invalid Access. A siren began to whoop.

"Security teams to level three B."

Defeat cackled in the background, and her inner kitty slashed at it until it retreated. There must be another way out. Air shafts. Lock picking. Speaking of locks...

Didn't doors with electronic access always have a manual override? She eyed the panel, inset within a frame, which, in turn, sat flush within the wall. What was behind it?

Let's find out. She popped claws from the tips of her fingers. Using the tips, she pried at the panel, hooking the metal. It held firm. She yelled in frustration and punched it.

It continued to flash red as it mocked her.

So she hit it again. And again and again until the door opened. One glimpse of the lizard dude standing in the cab with Andrew and she turned on her heel to bolt, knowing full well there was no escape. Didn't matter. She wouldn't just stand there and let them take her.

"Fetch her."

She ran faster, but it proved futile. A hand grasped at her hair, and she found herself screaming in pain as she was lifted off her feet. Fingers scrabbled at the scaled fist holding her aloft. The pain proved excruciating, and yet the horror at what capture meant hurt more.

Setting her on her feet, Fang paid her no mind as he strode back to the open elevator. She had to stumble after him lest he drag her. Tears of defeat pricked at her eyes, but that didn't mean they'd broken her fighting spirit.

"I'm going to rip your cojones off and stuff them with rice and spices before I eat them!"

And she'd eat them with pleasure.

Now before anyone judged her, keep in mind that, while human sensibilities might find themselves offended at such a cannibalistic threat, shifters weren't human. Not completely. Most of them lived with a predator sharing their mind, one that liked to hunt its food, kill it, and eat it. Usually raw.

Ugh. What could a girl do when her feline side wanted to rip into someone and make them into chunks of meat? At least manage to cook them before they got eaten.

By eating the enemy, I take on his strength. An old belief of her mother's that liked to rear its sage head every so often.

But Melanie's inventive suggestions on various ways of cooking psycho Fang's body parts did not loosen his grip. On the contrary, he got even more stupid as the blood north of his waist drained.

Apparently, feisty women who wanted to kill him for food acted as an aphrodisiac.

Eew. Turned out the crazy hunters did have a penis. It flopped out of his body from wherever it hid and poked at her.

"What is it with you and reptiles?" Andrew stated with disgust. "I should have known to steer clear of you when you broke up with Wes. I deserve better than that gator's leftovers."

"I deserved better, too," she muttered. "You were always lousy in the sack."

Expecting the slap, she managed to move her face with it, lessening the impact, but it still stung.

"Whore," Andrew spat.

"Tiny dick."

Slap.

Nice to know she still had a knack for pushing people's buttons. Even nicer to know she'd finally stopped kowtowing to Andrew the a-hole. She smiled through the pain as she taunted, "I had better orgasms masturbating."

But she didn't get a third smack.

A sneer distorted his features. "I see your game. You think you can anger me enough to hurt you so you don't have to participate in the next phase. Guess again. I'm going to be watching as you get taken by one of the special projects. It might even be Fang here."

The grunt behind her made her clamp her lips tight. Horror stole her breath.

The elevator trip proved thankfully short. As the doors slid open, she noted a long corridor, one she was forced into as Fang prodded her from behind.

Please let that be a finger and not something else.

Only a few doors lined this blank level. Nothing indicated its purpose. No signage, no windows to peek in, nothing.

The hallway employed recessed lighting behind solid steel cages. A precaution to prevent broken lights? Only someone expecting to piss off its prisoners would worry about that. The few doors on this level sat in thick metal frames, with embedded keypads alongside them.

For some reason, this area frightened her more than the line of cages. What horrors hid behind these benign portals? What torture would she have to survive?

And I will survive. Of that, she refused to have any doubt.

No matter what they did to her now, she needed to live so she could save her boys—*and shred that bastard, Andrew.*

Stopping before a door labeled Observation C, Andrew poked at the scanner but didn't swipe his wrist.

"Identify yourself," said a man.

I recognize that voice, she realized.

Her cat knew exactly who it was and pictured a man in a lab coat with glasses.

Dr. Philips. The one giving her fertility treatments.

Oh shit.

"It's Killinger. I've got the female."

"Excellent. The male is already inside waiting."

"What do you mean you already have a male? Who chose him?" Andrew asked.

"Parker did. He wants his nephew to have first crack at impregnating her."

Melanie felt a surge of relief. They wanted to put her with Wes? She could handle that.

"Why him?"

"It is not my place to question," Dr. Philips announced. "If you have a problem with it, then take it up with your partner. Now, if you're done questioning, get the female inside."

Displeasure creased Andrew's features, but he didn't argue further. "Before I open the chamber, is the male contained? I don't want any incidents."

"Pussy," she taunted.

Andrew smirked at her. "Perhaps you should show a little more fear, given you're about to be locked in a room with him. Did I forget to mention the gator might not be acting like himself?"

"What do you mean?"

"You didn't think we'd just want normal babies, did you? Wes has been given something a little extra to make this moment special."

With that, a door opened, and a rough shove sent her reeling in. She took a few stumbling steps before she could stop herself. Behind her, the door shut, and she heard the click of a lock engaging.

Great. Just fucking great. Anxious, she hugged herself and peeked around. There wasn't much to see. Four walls, padded in a strange substance. She pressed her fingers against it.

It squished, but when she dragged her nails across it, didn't even scratch.

The floor appeared to employ the same substance. It added a bounce factor to walking.

Embedded within another wall, the one at her back, she noted dark glass. Reflective on her side, showing a disheveled woman in a partially torn paper gown, her hair a frazzled disaster. She kept staring, the realization dawning that the glass acted as a viewing window.

People watched. Andrew watched. Which meant they expected a show.

She gave them one. Two slowly rotated digits and a smirk. They might hold the upper hand for the moment, but she'd not given up yet.

At a metallic cranking sound behind her, she whirled to see a section of the wall pulling apart. As the opening widened, a scent hit her.

Musty. Reptilian. Male. Wes. Another sniff and she could pinpoint another scent—violence. Madness.

Predators knew that smell. *Stay still,* her feline hissed.

While remaining still, she did peruse the now much larger space. With the dividing wall gone, the room proved rectangular in shape, long and narrow. Also dim. Very dim.

So dim that, at first, she didn't see the shadow at the far end.

Knowing it was Wes didn't ease her trepidation, not with the hint of violence in the air.

"Wes?"

No reply. The shadow stepped closer, a dark, hulking shape that brought a shiver to her skin.

"You're scaring me." An admission she hated to make, and yet, there was something in his slow advance, the way he moved, that frightened her.

I don't think Wes is home.

The alien scent drew nearer, and she didn't realize she backed away until her back hit the smooth glass wall behind her.

Fear thumped, an irregular stutter of her heart as her breath drew short and ragged.

Inside her head, her feline yowled. She wanted out. She wanted to stand strong in the face of this threat.

But poor kitty was locked in. Melanie had tried so many times on the way over, and nothing other than a pop of a few claws worked.

It was only her, a paper gown, and whatever Wes had become.

Which, as it turned out, was a walking, talking dinosaur.

And he grabbed her by the throat!

Chapter 18

HE HELD the female off the floor, high enough that he could properly peruse her. His mate appeared uninjured, and yet he could smell the fear rolling off her. He brought his snout close, inhaling her aroma, rubbing himself on her skin to mark her with his scent. Wearing a bull's mark would reassure the female that he would protect her against danger.

At least now he would. His pinker self might have had problems accomplishing the task, but he was stronger now. In control, too.

Such strength flowed through him. *I am the strongest.* And to him came the rewards along with the irritations.

A fly buzzed in his head. *Put her down. She's fragile, you big, dumb gator.*

No talking. I am in control.

For now. And only because of those drugs.

I am strong. I shall eat our enemies.

Yeah, well, if you're going to do that, then you need to

have a bit of patience because we're not getting out of this room until we do the deed.

The female requires insemination.

Let's try and not call it insemination. And you might want to let me drive for this part.

If I relinquish this part, you will let me have the hunt?

Yes.

We have a bargain. Snap.

The quick flash of thoughts between them took but a moment, as did the changes back to himself. Wes's more sane and human-looking self.

Along with his man skin came shame.

"Fuck." He couldn't help but curse as he released Melanie.

He waited for her to launch into him. He knew he would have with the roles reversed.

"Are you okay?" she asked.

The lack of freakout upset him more. "No." The single syllable a guttural grunt. No, he wasn't fucking okay. Neither was she. None of this was fucking okay.

He spun away from her, a few short strides removing him from the reminder of his failure.

I didn't save her, and now we're both stuck here.

"Argh!" He smacked the wall beside him with his fist, only to feel it sink and bounce back.

He leaned his head against the wall, breathing slowly, trying to come down from the fact that his colder side had taken over. Scarier, he'd had to cajole it into giving control back.

The injection, while not meant to change him—at

least according to the doctor—did, however, grant more strength to his inner beast.

Not necessarily a good thing.

"Might I remind you that time is wasting and you've yet to fuck her?" Parker's sly words emerged muffled in this strange place. For a moment, as his gator retook control of his motions, he peered around, looking for an enemy to chomp.

No one appeared. Cowards. It was only him and Melanie here.

A pity. He had some pent-up energy that needed expending.

"Do I need to find another male to take your place?" Parker threatened.

"No." As he spat the word, he pushed from the wall and walked stiff-legged back to Melanie. He stood over her, looming as he stared down. His skin prickled with awareness. He knew the window she leaned against hid watchers.

Leaning down, he bent far enough that his forehead touched hers. He breathed her scent in and heard the rapid flutter of her heart.

Still frightened, but also oozing a sense of anticipation. Did she know what would happen? Would she hate him for it?

"You don't have to do this," she said softly.

"You would rather do another?" He couldn't help the jealous accusation. It came from a primal part of him.

"What? No. I don't want to do this at all. You know what they are attempting. If we do this, then we play right into their hands."

"And if we don't, then you'll be forced by another. We don't have a choice, angel. I'm so sorry." He truly was. He took all the blame. Things might have gone differently if he'd acted that night when Andrew went to fetch her. That was the night everything truly started to go to shit.

Or why not go back further? If I'd not set her free all those years ago, then she and I would be together. And she might have never entered his uncle's or Andrew's radar.

Maybe gators will fly, his beast snorted.

Wait, they did.

Fuck.

"I'm waiting. Tick. Toc. Should I come in there and show you how it's done?" His uncle's taunt drew a rumbling growl from him, and he glared at the smoky glass, seeing only the terribleness of his eyes. The darker side of him swam close to the surface.

Soft hands cupped his cheeks and turned his gaze to her gentler one. "Ignore him."

"I wish I could."

"But you're right. We can't. So let's do it. Right now."

A grin threatened to pull his lips. "Isn't that what you said right before the first time we screwed?"

She smiled. "You remember."

"Of course I do. I never forgot anything about you." Not the way she clutched at him and cried out his name. The way she shyly admitted she loved him.

"Blah blah blah. Get the show on the road, nephew."

"Argh." He punched the glass, feeling the slight vibration from the impact. Stupid tempered shit. He wanted to smash through it and kill those watching on the other side. Instead, he could only sigh. "Sorry it came to this."

"Not entirely your fault. I mean, you didn't marry the douchebag that got me involved."

"That douchebag is watching," Andrew announced.

"Keep watching. Then maybe you'll see where you kept going wrong," she snapped.

Wes almost laughed. "You know that is just pulling his stubby tail."

"I don't care. What else can the bastard do to me?"

"Don't ask and don't tempt. And never forget it's a Mercer running things."

"And this Mercer"—she poked him in the chest —"will find a way to fix it. I know you will." Her faith in him didn't warm as much as the soft brush of her lips on his. She caught his mouth and sucked at his lower lip. Nibbled it.

What is she doing?

He knew this wasn't what she really wanted to do. Hell, he certainly didn't want her under these circumstances, but...

At what point did a man stop fighting the inevitable? This would happen, and in front of an audience.

But he could do his best at least to make sure they saw as little as possible.

Wes clutched Melanie in his arms, tucking her tight against his chest. He moved them, down to the middle of the room, the farthest from both viewing panes framing the space, in the deepest of the shadows because they didn't dare use proper lighting in here. No light bulbs, not even caged ones, lest they get used as a weapon.

The soft, phosphorous glow that came from the very walls and floor itself bathed Melanie in an unearthly sheen. He ran a knuckle down her soft cheek, the contrast of his rough, working hands against her smooth, tanned flesh a reminder of their differences. She grabbed his finger and sucked the tip, reminding him of the fact that they were so perfect together.

He leaned into her, his lower body pinning hers, his thin briefs unable to hide his erection. No matter the circumstances, he couldn't help but desire Melanie. He could make this good for her. Good for them both. He owed it to her in case it was their last chance.

The thought spurred him to action. He caught her lips with his, sucking at that lower one, catching the soft pants of her breath.

His hands skimmed her curves from the indent of her waist, the wide flare of her hips, then the curve of her thighs. The edge of her paper gown crinkled as he raised it. The palms of his hands stroked the silky flesh as he bared her, but in such a way that none could truly see.

She caught onto his idea and, bracing her hands on his shoulders, lifted her legs to lock them around his waist.

Their kiss deepened, her mouth parting for his tongue. He tasted her, thrusting his tongue into her mouth for a sinuous slide against hers. The erotic nature of the kiss thrilled him. Aroused him. Aroused his primal side.

Bite her.

He pushed the impulse down. He would do this as a man, not a beast.

Silky skin met his touch as he skimmed over her body, titillating her all without truly exposing her. It proved a torturous form of foreplay. He so wanted to drop to his knees and taste her. Stab his tongue between her velvety folds and taste her sweet honey. But they were watched.

Was it wrong to find arousal in that concept?

He whispered to her, "I want you so bad, but I don't want to hurt you." A man his size needed to prepare the way.

She clasped his hand and brought it between her legs. "Touch me."

Slick honey met his fingers as he stroked her mound. So hot. So wet.

Irresistible. Fuck those watching. This might be his last chance, her last chance, for pleasure. He dropped to his knees and tucked his head under her gown.

She parted her thighs for him, and the full impact of her scent hit him. He could have shot his load right then and there. He didn't, though. He preferred to hold back, to feel the pain of abstaining as he let his tongue dart forward and taste of her sweetness.

Pure fucking bliss. He suckled happily of her nectar.

It seemed some weren't happy at his actions. He vaguely heard a complaint of, "I thought he was supposed to fuck her." And, "If you can't handle watching, leave."

He didn't care. He lost himself in the scent and heat that was Melanie. His. *Mine.*

His tongue stroked her velvety folds, spreading them that he might stab his tongue inside her, feeling the tightness of her channel. She lifted a leg over his shoulder, granting him better access, and he used it to stroke the tip of his tongue over her clit.

A shudder rocked her frame, and a small gasp of his name, "Wes," slipped past her lips.

He stroked her faster, alternating tugs against her button, feeling her body quivering at his touch while her pulse raced erratically.

When she neared her peak, he stood. His erection throbbed within the confines of his briefs. He lifted her first, anchoring her against the wall. She locked her legs around his waist. He freed himself, only to have her reach between them to clasp him.

Tight fingers gripped around his cock. The urge to thrust his hips and come was so strong. But he knew a better place to bury himself.

He lifted her gown, pushing the paper liner out of the way. With her legs wrapped around his hips, none could see the tip of his cock probing at the pinkness of her sex. He watched as her channel hungrily gobbled his length. He pushed in, and she took, the heat of her squeezing all around.

She grabbed his head and drew him to her for a kiss. Their bodies pulled together tight, and all of him ended up sheathed in her welcoming heat.

Pure bliss. He moaned against her mouth. This shouldn't have felt so good. They came together because they had to. How could he take such pleasure?

Take it. Because who knew if he'd ever feel pleasure again.

He rotated his hips, pushing into her, driving the very tip of his cock deeper. So deep.

Her flesh squeezed him, much like a tight fist gripping him as he pushed in and out of her, driving her with his need, raising their arousal to a point where they both panted and glistened.

"I love you," she whispered against his mouth just as her body tensed.

"You shouldn't," was his reply. And then he could speak no more as he came. She came, too, with a sharp cry and undulating waves, the sweet flesh of her sex shuddering around him and drawing out his pleasure to a bittersweet point.

He might not want to admit it aloud, but he could, here, in this moment, in his head.

I love you, too, angel. So much that it hurt.

Chapter 19

REALITY WANTED TO INTRUDE. Melanie didn't want to let it. She refused to think about the fact that they'd made love in front of an audience. Refused to think about what would happen next.

She hugged Wes tight, as if by holding on she could keep the ugliness away.

It didn't work. "The subjects will move to opposite ends of the room," a man's voice ordered.

"Dr. Philips can kiss my ass if he thinks I'm leaving you. I'm not letting you out of my sight." Wes set her on her feet and smoothed down her pathetic excuse for a dress.

The words warmed, and yet, she couldn't help but wonder how Wes would manage to keep his promise. "What are we going to do?"

"Bust out of this joint."

Great optimism, but for one teensy problem. "How? In case you hadn't noticed, we're locked in a room."

"Yup."

"And?" she prodded.

"And I will get us out."

A heavy sigh blasted past her lips. "How?"

"Dare me," he said with a grin that didn't quite match the cold glint in his eye.

"Dare you?" she repeated.

"Yes, challenge me to get us out. I'm a Mercer. It's part of my genetic makeup to have to attempt it, no matter how impossible seeming."

"And how is challenging you going to change facts?"

"Because I'm a Mercer. I'll find a way."

"Enough chattering. There is no escape. You are in a sealed room. You will separate and move to opposite ends. Comply or I will release gas into the chamber."

Wes pivoted to face the glass window—tall, straight, and bristling. Danger hummed under his skin. "Are you really stupid enough to think for one minute I'd believe you'll gas us? Like hell you will. I know you, Dr. Philips. I know how desperate you are for your little project to succeed. You won't do anything that might risk your breeding experiment. Because, if you do, my uncle will have your balls."

An imp made Melanie add, "For dinner."

Wes tossed her a look, his lips twitching in an almost smile. "With hot sauce."

"You are not leaving that chamber until you are separated and contained. The longer you refuse, the longer you stay locked in there." Dr. Philips put on his sternest voice for his threat.

It left Wes unimpressed. "You want to leave us here? Sounds good to me."

It did? She quickly saw his logic. In there, together, at least, she could pretend some hope.

"You're being stubborn."

Wes cocked his head. "Just being a Mercer. Now, if you're done, go inject yourself with some more stupid shit. With any luck, you'll think you're a dog and decide your time is better spent playing fetch."

This time, she laughed out loud. The situation was dire, her life in jeopardy, but still, Wes was with her.

With her. Loving her. He might not have said as much, but he had to. Why else fight for her like this?

Dr. Philips made a sound that came close to a growl. "You won't get any food, water, or any other amenities until you obey."

Tapping his chin, Wes smirked. "No food? Are you sure about that?" He sniffed. A big, long whiff with his eyes shut that culminated in a wide, tooth-filled grin. "I smell coward behind that glass. It's not my preferred meal of choice, but a gator's got to eat."

"You can't get to me. This is bullet-proof glass."

"Never did much like that word can't. And I never could say no to a challenge." Wes flexed his arms, his skin rippling. "Stand back, angel. I think it's time we blew this joint."

Past time. She might have asked how he planned to get them, except she noted Wes began to morph, his control over the changes in his body astonishing. His torso widened, and thick scales rose from his skin, their color dark and dull out of water. The skin she'd so recently touched and admired turned into something else. Wes made himself into an armor-plated beast, which then ran on powerful legs at the glass.

Bang. He hit it shoulder first, the window absorbing most of the impact. Most being the key word. The window vibrated at the shock, and she heard the slight crackle of things straining.

"You can't get through."

Surely Wes heard the waver of uncertainty in those words. She did, and she could have laughed. The room surely was impenetrable—to normal people. Even difficult for most shifters to escape from. She'd wager the walls were concrete. The doors reinforced steel. But in wanting that window to watch the action, they'd created a weak spot. A weak spot not meant for a big, bad gator in a pissed-off mood.

Wham. The vibration went on longer this time it seemed as the glass shuddered.

Wes retreated and ran again as it still quivered.

The doctor screamed, "Stop!"

As if Wes would listen. *Bang.* He hit the glass again, and this time, it did more than shudder. He left behind a hairline crack.

The doctor stopped yelling. Not a good sign.

Wes took a few steps away from the window, readying for another rush. In the silence, she heard the hiss of escaping gas. "They're going to drug us!" she warned, taking a deep lungful of oxygen before it became contaminated.

Wes didn't reply. This dark beast had no expression. He charged again, ramming hard against the window with his shoulder. The single split fractured into a spider web of lines.

An alarm went off. *Whoop. Whoop.* The strident sound pierced her ears. But she didn't mind it because it meant Dr. Philips was scared.

He should be scared. Very scared because they were coming for him.

With his next bull gator rush, Wes smashed through. The hard ridge of his scales prevented him from getting sliced to ribbons. His armor also meant the dart the doctor fired at him bounced off.

"Ffffucker." Wes hissed the word as he lunged through the opening.

"Don't touch me," screamed the doctor, and surprisingly, she aped his words.

"Don't kill him. We need him alive to use the elevator."

"I'll save him," Wes grumbled, "as a snack for later."

The use of her air to talk meant her lungs burned. The gas swirled around Melanie as she fought not to breathe. She ran at the opening in the wall, reaching it just as Wes finished knocking out the sharp shards remaining.

He vaulted through and then turned to offer her a hand. She grasped it and let him pull her into the control room. She ignored the slumped body on the floor, gasping for air, feeling the tinge of the tranquilizer gas, acrid on her tongue.

The gas oozed into the room, overtaking the fresh stuff.

"We need out," she wheezed.

The door wouldn't yield to Wes's tug. She tapped his wrist, and he growled, "Duh," before grabbing the unconscious doctor and tossing him over a shoulder. Melanie held the doctor's wristband and then thumb against the scanner.

The door clicked open, and they stumbled into the hall, the gas trying to follow. She quickly slammed the door shut then turned at the *rat-tat-tat* of feet.

A pair of human guards ran toward them.

A roar erupted from Wes.

The guards replied by dropping to their knees and firing.

Wes immediately threw himself in front of Melanie. The darts fired fell harmlessly to the floor. As Wes advanced on the men, Melanie realized she couldn't keep hiding behind Wes.

I'm not a coward. But she could use some help from a certain feline.

Here kitty, kitty. Can you come out and play?

Ever since that last shot in her cell, she'd noted her senses coming alive. Could feel a certain vibration in her body that let her know she was returning to normal. She'd managed to pop some claws, but was that all?

Time to see if she could shift.

Ready?

Meow! Her panther burst out in an exuberant rush of fur and fangs, scattering the remnants of her paper gown. Power coursed through her limbs. Strength as well. With a push of hind legs, she bounded down the hall, snarling at the humans with wide, white eyes. Eyes that stared blankly once she bowled into them.

Keep me prisoner will they?

Rawr!

She kept on running past the downed guards, the other half of her reminding the alarm would draw more of the humans with their weapons.

Squeaky toys. Yay.

Dangerous, her more logical self reminded.

Yes, dangerous, with their weapons that fired those things that made her want to sleep. At least they were firing darts and not bullets. But that might not last long once the enemy realized she and Wes were on the loose.

The elevator doors slid open just as they arrived. The guards sporting real guns never stood a chance. They didn't even have time to scream as she leaped on one and Wes thundered into the other. Between the two of them, she slashed her foe into silence while her mate crushed the weaker body.

We make a formidable pair. No wonder their enemy Parker wished to mate them. Their children would be stupendous.

As the elevator door closed, shutting them in the box that moved, her fur remained hackled. Anger made her twitch. Someone had tried to lock her away. That male, the one she'd had as mate, tried to do her harm.

And they took my cubs.

She planned to get them back.

The doors opened and surprised those standing outside. Wes tossed the body of the human he carried at the guards, sending most falling to the floor. As for the one that dodged to the side and dared to raise his weapon?

With a snarl, she leaped and took him down. It proved messy, another layer of grime on her lush fur, but she'd have to groom herself later. They hadn't escaped yet.

No escape until we locate the cubs.

Their last location put them at the top floor. However, she and the gator appeared stuck on the main level. The elevator doors had sealed shut and wouldn't open, no matter whose wrist and thumb Wes slapped against the scanner.

Let me back out.

Her cat relinquished control, and Melanie shifted back, welcoming the painful reshaping of her bones as a sign that at least part of her was back to normal.

Wes remained in his hybrid shape. She couldn't have said how. She'd heard that, while it was possible to maintain a half shift, only a few could manage it. The strength of will required too much for most.

"What should we do?" She truly was at a crossroads of dilemmas. She needed to locate her boys, and yet, if she stayed, she would run the high risk of getting captured again. Maybe killed.

On the other paw, if she escaped, she could go for help, but would she get back in time to save her boys?

Instead of replying, Wes's head lifted.

She heard it a moment later, too. The crack and pop of gunfire.

"What the hell?" she muttered, taking a few steps toward the windows at the front of the building.

An explosion rocked the floor under their feet. The whooping alarms trebled in reply.

A glance through the glass windows of the lobby for the research building showed people running and screaming, but more interesting, smoke billowed in the distance by the front gate.

"What's happening?" she asked.

A computer voice announced, "Perimeter breach. All personnel please lock down your workstations. Security forces to the gate. This is not a drill." *Whoop. Whoop.*

It would have proven fascinating—in a movie! Being a part of what sounded like guerilla warfare? Kind of freaky, especially when Wes exclaimed, "Stay here. I'll go look."

Wes charged through the glass, the more decorative windows on this floor easier to break than that several levels below.

She thought about following, and yet... She stared at the ceiling, wondering if her missing boys had left the building. Given how hard it was to get in and out, could they have taken her advice and hidden where no one could find them?

How could she go and look?

The elevator doors dinged open, but the cab appeared empty. She dove into the elevator and slapped at the console to shut them. *Move, do something.* But the screen flashed red and mocked her with the word, "Lockdown."

But there was more than one way to go up. She peeked at the ceiling. While hard to distinguish, it was there. Just like in every movie. A hatch. It took her jumping a few times, banging it, to push it to the side then another leap to grab the edges and haul herself through.

Once inside the shaft, she peeked up, way up. A metal-rung ladder embedded in the concrete provided a method to climb.

As she stared at the daunting climb, the whooping alarm cut out. In the new silence, her ears rang a bit with the echo of the strident call. Fingers gripping the metal, she climbed, trying to ignore the distant sound of gunfire. What happened outside? Was it the good guys, come to rescue?

Or had Bittech drawn the attention of enemies? Their kind long feared humanity's discovery. If they knew monsters walked among them, would they move to rid themselves of a perceived threat?

She didn't even want to contemplate a world where their kind might get hunted.

Never hunted. We are the dominant species. They are only prey.

A very simple animal reaction, an outdated one. Today's humans didn't keep things fair by fighting with only their body. They used knives, spears, and, most deadly of all, guns.

All the skill in the world couldn't help if someone shot a shifter long range.

Please let this be a rescue. Let this nightmare end. Let her find her babies.

Keeping her boys in mind, she clambered up the ladder, the adrenaline of doing something powering her movement. She only slowed at the top, stumped initially by the closed doors. Now what?

Open them. Put a little muscle into it.

Smart-ass cat. But her feline was right. *I can open these.* Before, she'd found herself unable to pry them open, the surface seamless with nothing to grip. But they'd not paid as close attention within the shaft.

The tips of her claws wedged in the seam, she took a few deeps breaths before straining. It took a bit of grunting, a few muttered choice words—including "open, you fucking piece of scrap metal." They finally opened when she talked about taking a blowtorch to them and melting them into a puddle. A gaping portal didn't mean she immediately dove through. Wanting to live meant acting smart.

Breath held, she stood to one side of the open doorway and listened.

"Who's there?" a female voice asked.

Could Melanie be so lucky? She couldn't help a feral grin as she stepped out and saw the human nurse she'd first met. The one she didn't like.

What must Nurse Bitch think as Melanie stalked naked from the elevator, body covered in blood. "Where are my children?"

The nurse's complexion paled as she backed away. "I don't know where those demon spawn are. They disappeared."

"Did you seriously call my children demon spawn?" Melanie arched a brow and smiled. "Thank you. But don't think compliments will save your life."

"Don't come near me." The nurse pulled out a needle. A wee one.

Melanie laughed. "Let's play cat and mouse. Guess which one I am?"

Even in her human guise, Melanie could move quickly. She also knew how to fight dirty. A quick jabbing left that hit a jaw. A grasp of a flailing arm. A twist of a wrist to get a certain needle dropped. More twisting to get the woman to drop to her knees.

"I am going to ask you one more time." She applied a little more pressure, even as the nurse whimpered. "Where are my children?"

"I told you. I don't know."

"Then you are of no use to me." At the moment. Melanie snagged the discarded needle and jabbed the nurse with it, sending her into instant sleep. Killing her wasn't an option yet. She might need the nurse's active wristband and thumb to get out. With her boys.

Once she found them.

Chapter 20

RUSHING out of the medical building, Wes found himself immersed in noise, out-of-place noise that took a moment to process.

Under the whooping wail of the siren, he could hear the crackle of gunfire as weapons were discharged. Smoke curled with wispy tendrils in the air at a distance. Yells, screams, and even the roars and snarls of animals filled the air. More surreal was the golf cart that went whipping past, a pair of guards holding on for dear life. On their tail? A galloping moose.

He blinked. Yeah, still a moose with a big fucking rack chasing the shrinking cart.

By the time he saw the polar bear and the caribou, nothing could surprise him.

Was he hallucinating from the drugs pumped into the observation room? It might explain the madness around him.

A guttural roar saw him looking to his left. He wasn't

surprised to see a big brown bear taking on one of the scaled hunters. It seemed the creatures were loose. He noted more than one monstrosity diving and flapping in the sky.

What of his brother? Was Brandon among them? He'd not seen nor heard of his brother since his capture. What did that mean?

The vicious snarls of the Kodiak and the lizard snapped him back to the present. He really should help, even if the bear seemed as if he was doing a fine job. He danced away from the claws that might poison him. He kept clear of the slavering jaws. The Kodiak also had help in the form of a massive timber wolf nipping at the heels of the dinoman.

What should he do? He'd left Melanie inside, but he'd not had time to ensure it was secure. Wes had to trust Melanie could take care of herself while she awaited his return. A return that was delayed as a black panther leaped from the top of a careening SUV to land in front of him with a snarl.

Wes only knew of one family of cats in the neighborhood. Forcing himself to release his hybrid gatorman shape, he stood before Daryl, hands cupping his junk because it was never wise to dangle things in front of irate kitties.

For a moment, Daryl paced in front of him, peeling back his lip for an angry noise. He did that a few times before morphing into his human shape, a human shape resembling that of a very angry Latino male, who punched him in the face without warning.

"Asshole! Where the fuck is my sister?"

Hit him back, his gator advised as Wes rotated his jaw. Melanie's brother packed an impressive punch. But he wouldn't return it. Melanie wouldn't like it, and that mattered to him. "Melanie's still inside the building. I didn't want to bring her out until I knew what was happening."

"Retribution has arrived," Daryl replied with some pride.

"Those your friends?" he asked, jerking a thumb at the polar bear who cuffed a grizzly, who then proceeded to head-butt the furball until they both shifted shapes and stood glaring nose to nose. Only to laugh a second later.

The camaraderie of good friends. Other than Brandon, Wes had given up on that years ago, but he missed it.

"They're friends. Allies. Call them what you like. They're part of the rescue team."

"How did you know where to come?" It was possible someone from Bitten Point had followed them, yet unlikely. Andrew and Parker took many precautions, precautions that seemed unfounded, given their open flaunting of shifters in and around the compound. "Did my sister make it out to tell you?" Wes asked.

He'd not spoken to Brandon since his capture. For all he knew, his brother had made it out of here with their sibling.

"Your sister? She's here, too?" Daryl couldn't hide a genuine inflection of surprise.

Deflation sucked some of the hope out of him. "If Brandon and Sue-Ellen didn't get out to tell you, then how did you find us?"

"My idiot little sister swallowed a tracker before taking her stupid ass off."

"Melanie wanted to save her boys."

"She should have told me what she was planning and we could have better prepared," Daryl grumbled.

As if. Melanie was too stubborn and brave for that. "Took you long enough to come for her," Wes noted.

A scowl crossed the other man's face. "I would have been here sooner, but Caleb and the others made me wait for backup."

Gesturing at the caribou racing around with a screaming guard on his rack and the moose who stood watching with evident disgust, Wes said, "Interesting help."

"I know. Not my friends. Apparently, Caleb knew a couple guys, mostly army dudes, from Kodiak Point."

Wes couldn't help his surprise. "Up in Alaska? And they came down here?"

"Them plus all the able-bodied folk in our town. And a few others. Once they all heard what was happening, no one could ignore it."

Knowing Daryl had come with enough aid to truly shut this place down lightened Wes's heart, and yet, at the same time, something niggled. Wes had left Melanie alone for more than a few minutes. Who the hell knew what kind of trouble she'd get into?

"I gotta go find Melanie."

"I'll come with you."

At least that was the plan when Daryl began loping back with him to the building until the sound of a chopper overhead distracted.

The news logo on the side almost made him trip. Wes recovered and darted into the building, wondering if anyone on board filmed his naked butt sprinting.

What were they doing here? It hadn't been long enough since the attack started for anyone to have reported the smoke or movie-style shoot-'em-up action. Had someone tipped them off?

This could get ugly, as in ditch-everything-behind-and-start-over-somewhere-new ugly. Another thing to worry about.

I'll have to watch the news later. After he found Melanie, who, of course, hadn't stayed where he left her.

It didn't prove hard to follow her scent. It went straight into trouble. He stared up the long shaft of the elevator and sighed.

Why couldn't shit ever happen in the bayou? He could swim great in there. Scuttle across the marsh lightning quick. Sneak attack. But climbing? That was for the lighter limbed.

But it took only a hollered, "Don't touch my mama!" for him to get moving.

I'm coming. In a zillion, billion rungs. *Ugh.*

Chapter 21

THE NURSERY LEVEL muffled the sounds of battle coming from outside, but she still heard them. The temptation to find a window to peek out of proved strong, but not as strong as Melanie's mommy instinct to find her babies.

On bare feet, Melanie padded the empty halls, straining for any sound or clue as to their location. The stillness in the air felt unnatural.

Inside, her inner kitty paced, and the sense of danger bristled her fur. *Don't trust the quiet,* her feline advised.

No worries on that count. The whole floor held a quality, that certain something, that let her know all was not as peaceful as it seemed. It was more than a gut instinct. She could feel it because buildings, places, they absorbed things and then oozed them. Right now, this twisted nursery oozed the calm before shit happened.

The smart move would be to leave, now. Find Wes. Find help. Do something. This level appeared abandoned, not a peep from her boys or anything else living, nothing except for that pervasive sense of danger.

I can't leave. What if my boys are still around here? At their size, they could hide anywhere. She would know. She'd almost lost her fur entirely more than once when they seemingly just disappeared.

Such as the time one peeked at her from a shelf in the closet behind spare linen. That fright took one of her lives.

The naughty little demon that popped up from the linen basket from under dirty clothes made her scream— and she lost another.

High entertainment for her boys and now, with danger stalking them, a honed skill that hopefully helped keep them out of harmful hands.

How to find them? Melanie didn't have time for a thorough search. But how else to find them when, as she walked, she couldn't help but taste the bitter ammonia in the re-circulated air. Its stringent scent nullified all others.

Forget scent. If she couldn't see or touch the boys, what did that leave?

Let's see if you're listening, babies. "Ollie, Ollie, oxen free," she sang, the universal song from her childhood for when they played hide-and-seek. "Come out. Come out, wherever you are." *Come out because Mama is here and I will keep you safe.*

She yodeled again to let her children know she'd arrived in case they remained on this level.

Good plan, and we'll let any enemies know we're here, too, so we can take care of them. Rowr.

She didn't correct the bloodthirsty plan. Anyone who got between her and her boys was asking for it. However, she doubted she'd really see much action. During her previous stay on the nursery level, she'd not seen any regular guards floating around, just the one nurse, and that bitch currently snored at the front desk.

Past the nurses' station, she got to peek down the long hall lined with doors and windows. It seemed all the rooms were open. How strange. They'd always been locked before when she'd tried to get in them.

Given she figured her boys had either disappeared from the playroom or the barrack room with beds, she headed to the closest one first.

The playroom door teased with its wide opening. Easing along the wall, she halted for a moment to listen before she peeked in to see it looked like a tornado had gone through the room.

A tornado or a lizard? Even with the antiseptic smell in the air, traces of that psycho reptile lingered, as did his actions. Tables torn from the floor and overturned. Chairs thrown against walls, some smashed. Around the ventilation grills, the flooring and the plaster on the walls showed signs of damage. She wondered if the gaping holes were part of the search for Rory and Tatum? Just how crazy did Andrew and his people go looking? And how had her boys vanished?

Not seeing her sons in the room didn't mean she took off right away. She decided to look closer at the ripped openings just in case she found her babies tucked inside. Tatum had once made it into the attic and popped his legs through the vent in the bathroom.

Andrew had been less than impressed, seeing as how he was in the shower at the time and screamed like a girl. A scream Tatum kept, unfortunately, mimicking.

Sob. Please let my babies be okay. She missed them so much. She feared so hard for their safety. The best sign? There was no blood.

By the rip in the flooring, she dropped to her knees and peeked in the hollow and narrow space. No way had Rory or Tatum squeezed in there. Not only was the vent much too small, the area around the conduits was much too small to move through unless they were the size of a hamster.

Moving on, she noted the walls also didn't provide any clues, the steel plate underneath a solid barrier.

So where are they?

She stepped into the middle of the room and inhaled deeply. Once again, that stupid ammonia smell permeated, wiping all essences except the truly strong one of the lizard thing known as Fang. Had they unleashed that crazy bastard after her babies? Had he found and hurt them?

He better not have.

The reminder she wasn't there to protect them angered her. Claws popped from her fingers, and the hair all over her body prickled.

This is Andrew's fault. His and Parker's. They took my babies. She would kill them for that.

She stepped back out into the hall, first taking a peek to ensure it remained clear.

Outside the building, the crackle and pops of gunfire had pretty much ceased, and she no longer heard the vicious barks and roars of the animal kingdom gone to war. She did, however, hear the *whup-whup-whup* of an approaching helicopter.

I must move more quickly.

A few strides and she arrived at the gaping door to the sleeping room. Her heart stuttered at the sight of the mussed bunks. In here, she could smell her sons. Smell their little-boy scent.

None of the destruction of the playroom had made it to this place. A walk around the perimeter didn't reveal any clues or other exits. If her boys were here, she couldn't have said where. A peek under the bunks didn't reveal anyone.

"Where are you?" she muttered.

"Right here."

She whipped around at the words, a feral smile stretching her lips as she realized who stood in the doorway. "Andrew. Just the man I wanted to see." Wanted to see dead, but she didn't specify that. He'd learn first-paw soon enough.

"Looking for the brats?"

"Where did you put my sons?" A rumbly growl accented her query.

An irritated scowl crossed his face. "Nowhere. They disappeared. From a locked room no less."

"They escaped." She couldn't help a spurt of elation. Now if only she could be sure they'd escaped this place entirely because she couldn't wait to leave.

First, though, she needed to ensure the man before her didn't live long enough to ever harm her boys again.

"Are you gonna run and make this sporting for me?"

she asked with a swing of her hips as she walked toward Andrew. She was done catering to his little ego—and she meant little. Her cat hovered, waiting for a chance to leap forth.

"We'll see who does the running. I'm a changed man now." As he spoke, his voice changed. It dipped deeper. He began to sprout hair, coarse brown and black strands, and yet he kept his human shape. He also kept his face, if hairier, but his eyes, they glinted a dark orange, and they glowed from within, alight with madness and violence. "I am so tired of people thinking they're bigger and better than me. Especially you. You always made me feel small."

"You never could grasp it wasn't about size. All you had to do, Andrew, was believe in yourself. To stand tall."

"I'm standing tall now." He certainly was, as his body pushed upward and thickened. How was he doing this? Animals were restricted by the size of the host. Big men turned into big creatures. They were also heavy men as humans. But still, certain laws applied.

They just didn't seem to apply to Andrew. He stood about eight feet tall. His body kept its human shape, despite his freakish size and fur.

She should also mention the honking huge claws. While over his shoulders peeked... She gasped. "Wings?"

But Andrew didn't seem too interested in answering her surprise. With a roar of primal rage, he charged at her. She leaped out of the way, changing mid-air, a skill she'd learned as a cub because of an older brother determined to teach her to protect herself. Daryl used to practice by tossing her in the pond behind their house. She quickly learned to flip in mid-air and land with four paws on the one rock projecting from the surface. She hated getting her feet wet.

She also hated things that wanted to eat her. As Andrew rushed past, she landed behind him and slashed with her paw, her own claws extended.

Score! The cuts oozed dark red. A victory she couldn't bask in because Andrew had already turned around. Snorting, much like a bull, his eyes seemed to get darker. He came at her again.

As her feline, Melanie could spring and dodge with ease, but Andrew possessed a long reach. The tip of a sharp nail caught her, and she screeched at the sudden bright flare of pain against her rear haunch.

It was then that a blanket flew off a bed, and from a hollowed-out spot in the mattress, a little body came flying out, arms and legs spreadeagle.

"Don't you touch my mama!" Rory yelled.

He hit the papa bear and clung like a monkey, his little fists pummeling. So heartbreakingly brave, so woefully small. Andrew immediately plucked her son and held him out, short limbs kicking and punching.

A low, menacing rumble oozed from her, the intent clear—*Don't hurt my baby*.

Andrew roared and shook Rory.

Oh, hell no. She wanted to leap at Andrew, tear him to shreds, but she had to tread carefully. The man held her cub's life in his paw.

She took slow, slinking steps toward them, her gaze unwavering. As center of attention, Andrew let a parody of a grin stretch his misshapen features. He pulled Rory close and inhaled deeply. Then licked his lips.

A horrifying threat that her son understood. He hung from Andrew's grasp like a scolded puppy. Limp. Head hanging.

My poor baby. Mama's here. I won't let him hurt you.

She caught a glimpse of her son's eyes through thick, dark hair. Mischief gleamed, and he winked.

What. The. Hell? She couldn't even scream, *Don't do it.* There was no time. Rory flipped from feigned terror to rabid kitty. He flipped in the air, using the hand holding him as a pivot point. He managed to lock his little legs around Andrew's neck while, at the same time, landing a bite.

A fantastic move on anyone else, not an eight-foot, mutant freak.

Andrew snapped a gasket, yanking her son away and shaking him, hard.

He shook her child. Shook. Him.

I will shake you. Once she clamped him in her jaws. She'd whip him around like a rag doll for daring.

Rowr. Her roar vibrated in the air, challenging the bear in front of her who dared threaten her cub.

"Don't move," grunted the Andrew-thing. "Or the brat dies."

At that threat, Tatum appeared, standing on the bed to Andrew's left. Rory lifted his head, his eyes still not cowed. In twin tandem, her babies replied to Andrew's threat. "But don't you love us, Daddy?"

The boys didn't know, and Melanie wasn't about to

hide the truth from them. She shifted back to her human form. "Andrew is not your daddy."

"Then we don't have to be nice anymore," Tatum announced as he dove at Andrew's legs.

"Hate him," announced Rory, who swung suddenly, his two little feet connecting with Andrew's less-than-impressive family jewels.

Teetering on one leg, and thrown off balance, Andrew fell, and she could only watch in fascination as her darling twins, who should have been unable to shift yet being so young, turned into something feline, yet scaled.

Oh my.

Her twin terrors nipped at the monster, instinct controlling their actions.

But Andrew wasn't done with the surprises. With a massive roar, he flung their little bodies from him and stood. And he grew. Grew even bigger. His eyes turned a complete red, and he huffed. "Meat."

Um, no.

Time to get out of here.

Chapter 22

AS HE EMERGED from the elevator shaft, it took only a quick glance to see nobody was in sight. Wes immediately sprinted for the hall. How frustrating during the seemingly interminable climb to hear the signs of a fight and yet be so far.

But he'd arrived, and as he bolted toward the corridor past the nurses' station, he skidded to a halt as he spotted a naked and bloody Melanie racing up the hall, one scaled cub boy on her hip, the other loping on all four, his yellow eyes ablaze.

Behind them galloped a monster. Holy fuck, what was that?

Part bear, part bat, part insanity. Whoever and whatever it was, Wes had to stop it.

"Shoot it!" she screamed.

As if he had a gun hidden on his naked ass. "Get into the elevator shaft. I'll slow it down." Because killing a thing that size might prove a little challenging.

Challenge? His inner beast perked. *We are stronger than Andrew.*

This was Andrew? How did his beast know?

As Melanie raced past him, she confirmed it. "Andrew's taken some kind of drug. Whatever it is, it's made him hard to hurt. And huge."

Great. A really big challenge for this gator.

Ready?

Stupid question. His gator surged forth, pushing Wes out of the way, wanting this fight, wanting to test himself in this battle of will and strength.

At the sight of his gator, a gator that seemed larger than even Wes recalled, the charging monster slowed and halted. At the junction of hall and reception area, Andrew paced, head low to the floor as he circled slowly, his nose twitching as it tested the air. *Snuffle. Snort. Grunt.*

Wes didn't know what the monster did, but he also didn't want to spook it quite yet, so he didn't move from his spot in front of the elevator shaft. Melanie needed time to get down with her boys to safety. She was going to get that time.

And maybe a new fur rug.

His slitted eyes tracked the mutant bear as it crept closer. The reach on those paws was insane, the clawed tips rendering them even more deadly.

The leathery wings at its back fluttered, but given their stunted size, Wes doubted they provided any real use.

He heard excited yells from the shaft at his back. The echo moving upwards from some place low.

Melanie and the boys made good time in their descent.

They're safe.

Time for him to deal with Andrew and then join them.

Wes opened his mouth wide in invitation. Then clacked it shut. Snap. The message was clear. *Come and get me, asshole.*

Andrew lunged, but Wes was ready for it. He scuttled to the side and whipped around, jaws chomping at a hairy hindquarter. A major roar erupted as he scored a bite.

Wes sidestepped as Andrew whirled and slammed a fist down. Smash. Smash. Left fist, right fist. Both cracking tile.

Before Andrew could pull upright, Wes darted in and grabbed hold of Andrew's wrist. He locked his teeth around it and tried not to gag on the hairball in his mouth. Ugh.

A normal creature would have freaked and tried to pull free. Normal being the key word. Andrew was way past that point, and he proved freakishly strong. The Andrew monster lifted his arm and dangled fucking Wes from it. Shook him, too.

You are not getting rid of me that easily. Wes held on tight, even when he got slammed into the wall alongside the elevator shaft.

That smarted.

So he bit harder, feeling sinew and flesh tearing, the acrid blood of his enemy coating his tongue. Revolting and definitely not the yummy flavor of something freshly hunted. The blood tasted wrong, and that was the reason why Wes finally relinquished his grip. He wanted to spit the foulness from his mouth. Needed to rid himself of the vile taint that numbed his tongue.

Andrew took it as a sign he won. The mutant freak pounded his chest and roared. Enamored of his supposed superiority, Andrew never looked down. Never saw Melanie as she reached from the elevator shaft and grabbed his leg for a yank.

She didn't have enough weight to make it work, and before Andrew could react, Wes propelled himself forward as fast as he could.

Smack. He plowed into Andrew's hairy legs, and the teeter turned into a totter, and then gravity gave them a hand.

Down the shaft Andrew fell, bellowing, his stunted wings flapping, arms and legs pedaling. None of it helped.

Thunk.

The sound of Andrew's body hitting the elevator roof made the whole shaft tremble.

Speaking of tremble, he could see Melanie's arms shook where she held on to the lip of the door. Quickly, Wes shifted shapes, determined to grab her. A quick roll on the floor and he snagged her wrists before she went elevator shaft diving.

Their eyes met.

"Hi," she said.

Happiness at her safety flooded him, but the only thing he could think of saying was, "You were supposed to escape with your boys."

"Daryl has them."

"And he let you come back?"

"In his defense, I didn't tell him I was. They were all kind of distracted by the helicopter outside filming them."

Shit. The news chopper. Not good. Not good at all. "We need to get out of here before that news clips hits the air."

"Then what are you waiting for?" She smirked.

"For you to move that sweet ass out of the way."

In the end, he helped her with that ass, her adrenaline finally having peaked during the battle. She clung to him, arms and legs wrapped around his body as he clambered down.

As he neared the bottom, they couldn't help but note the body atop the elevator, a body now shrunken and pink skinned again. The body also wasn't quite dead. The chest rose and fell, and a wheezing rattle whistled through Andrew's lips.

As Melanie and Wes hopped onto the roof of the elevator cab, Andrew opened bloodshot eyes. "Fucking bitch. I should have killed you when I had the chance."

"That would have taken balls." Melanie glanced at Andrew's groin. "And we both know how lacking you are in that department."

"My father will kill you for this."

"Your father hasn't been seen in days," Wes reminded. "He knew the end was coming and got out."

"Liar."

"Doesn't really matter, does it?" Wes crouched down

on one knee. "You'll be dead in a matter of minutes. You lost."

A chuckle rattled from Andrew's broken body. "Did I really lose? My legacy will live on in my creations. Even you can't escape the taint, gator. It runs in your veins now and in that of your sons."

Wes assumed Andrew spoke to Melanie, and yet why did the man never break their stare?

"Stupid fucking gator. You still don't get it, do you?" Andrew's attempt at another chuckle turned into a wet cough. Blood filmed his lips. "The boys are yours. And you never even knew it."

With that final shocker, Andrew died, his eyes staring sightlessly above.

Wes might have died a little in that moment, too.

Holy fuck, I'm a dad.

Snap. His chin hit the top of the elevator as he slumped forward.

Chapter 23

WHAT'S WRONG WITH WES? A flutter of panic swept Melanie as Wes keeled forward moments after the news he was actually the father of the twins.

Mine and Wes's. How could I have not guessed? Then again, why would Melanie ever have thought them anything other than Andrew's, given the elaborate hoax her supposed husband perpetrated all those years.

If Andrew wasn't already dead, she'd kill him again.

Or maybe she should thank him. At least her sons wouldn't have to grow up thinking their dad was a psychotic murderer. Now they could have a dad who was just a psychotic gator.

The mind-blowing reality would have to wait, though. Something ailed Wes. He'd yet to move since he'd plunked face-first.

Please let him be okay. She sank beside him on her bare knees and turned him over to check him for signs of injury. She didn't see any obvious wounds, only a few bruises and scratches. Had someone poisoned him? Those crazy doctors were pretty liberal with their use of drugs and needles.

She cupped his cheeks, reassured that he at least breathed. "Wes! Wes!"

As she shouted his name, his eyes fluttered open, the ridiculously long lashes framing them so beautifully. "Angel? Is that really you? Am I in heaven?"

"No, you idiot. You're still on the elevator giving me a scare. What's wrong with you?" Please let it be something not fatal. She didn't think she could handle losing Wes again.

"I'm a daddy," he uttered with incredulity.

She blinked at his words. "Yeah. You're a daddy. To twins terrors, I might add. But I asked you what's wrong with you."

He repeated himself. "Fuck me, I'm a daddy." With that, he closed his eyes again.

He's freaking out because he's a father? She gaped at him. She also slapped him.

That got him wide-awake and glaring. "What did you do that for?"

"You're a daddy. Get over it. No need to go all fainting princess on me."

"I am not fainting. I am merely resting my eyes and processing events."

"Well, process them later. Weren't you the one saying we had to get out of here? I'm expecting the cops will show anytime now. I don't know about you, but I'd rather not explain why I'm naked and covered in blood."

"There's no way we're going to be able to keep this

hidden," he said, scrambling to his feet. "If they even taped half of what happened, there are going to be questions. Lots of them."

She couldn't help but agree. "The kitty is out of the bag, and I don't think there's any hope of stuffing it back in. But that doesn't mean we should stick around and wait for shit to happen. I, for one, don't want to get stuffed back into another cage."

"Good point. Let's get out of here."

She could have snorted as he suddenly went from Mr. Limp Noodle to Mr. Decisive. Wes shoved Andrew's body to the side, away from the opening. He leaped down first, took a peek, declared, "All clear," and then held up his arms for her.

Unnecessary. She could have jumped down on her own, but she did appreciate the gesture.

His callused hands caught her around the waist as she hopped down through the opening. He lowered her slowly, letting her body rub against his during the descent. She couldn't help a shiver of desire. Nothing like skin-to-skin touch to remind her she lived.

Wes clutched her close and buried his face in her messy hair. "Is it wrong to want to hold you forever and keep you safe?"

Not wrong, and it did all kinds of crazy things to her heart. She hugged him. "Let's plan on hugging like this again later. Naked. If you're good," she teased, and that was if they got out of here. Let her promise be the incentive he needed to get them to safety because, even with Andrew dead, they weren't out of the woods and safe in the bayou yet.

Emerging from the elevator, she noted a large sports utility vehicle out front. Her brother leaned against it, wearing only track pants while talking to another big guy, also only in pants. Being raised as a shifter meant she knew not to stare at all the bare flesh, and they extended the same courtesy. She exited and caught the T-shirt he tossed at her.

"Where are the boys?" she asked as she tugged the fabric over her head.

"Safe thanks to their most excellent uncle." Daryl growled. "What happened to stay put, don't move? I turned my back for one freaking second and you were gone."

"Wes needed me."

"Did not," Wes refuted. "I had things perfectly under control."

"Whatever."

Daryl clapped his hands. "Argue about it later and get in the truck. We're about to have company. Someone called in the media and the cops and anyone else who ever wanted to join a three-ring fucking circus."

"I can't leave without my sister or brother," Wes announced, yanking on a pair of gray track pants.

"Where are they?"

Just as Wes pointed to the building housing Parker, an explosion trembled the ground underfoot and the windows blew out. Smoke immediately followed, as did more explosions as, one by one, the buildings imploded.

"Move!" Daryl yelled, shoving her toward the truck.

She understood his haste. If someone had set off

bombs to get rid of evidence, then the medical institute would probably go next.

Sliding into the backseat of the truck, she didn't make it far before little arms, poking from oversized shirts, grabbed at her.

"Mama!" the twins yelled, crushing her in their exuberance. She loved it and squished them right back.

My boys. They're safe. Tears pricked at her eyes.

"Move over, angel. Make room." Wes climbed into the back seat with them, and he'd no sooner shut the door when the SUV sped off, Daryl in the passenger seat, a stranger at the wheel. Just in time, too. The biggest explosion of all made the whole world vibrate, and something hit the top of the truck hard enough to leave a dent.

"Fuck me, that was close," Daryl exclaimed.

"Yup," said the fellow behind the wheel.

"Who are you?" Wes asked, grabbing the T-shirt Daryl handed him from the bag he pulled it from in the front.

"Our driver is Boris," said her brother. "Dude with the big rack." To which Boris grunted.

"Thanks for coming out."

Melanie could have screamed at the polite exchange. "Say thank you later. I want to know what's happening."

"What's happening is the end of shifter civilization as we know it," Daryl announced.

"What do you mean the end?" she asked, and Daryl hesitated as he shot Wes a look.

Her brother sighed. "You want to explain it, or shall I?"

"I'll do it." Wes angled his head to face her. "Remember, angel, how we talked in the elevator shaft about how the cat's out of the bag? When Daryl says it's the end, what he means is our old lives are gone. We can't go back to Bitten Point, angel. None of us. What just happened back there? It's not going to get swept under a rug or ignored. People filmed us. Hell, we're probably being followed right now."

The warning saw her hugging the twins tighter. "So, what do you think is going to happen? Are we going to get hunted down?" Treated like animals instead of people?

His expression bleak, Wes shrugged. "Maybe. Depends what kind of spin the press puts on our existence."

"Where are we supposed to go?"

It was her boys who answered, "On an adventure."

Their optimism put some things in perspective.

I'm alive. They're alive. They might not be one hundred percent normal, but they were her babies. *Mine and Wes's.*

In a day filled with danger and surprises and death, it turned out the boys hadn't lost a daddy. They might have gained a real one.

If a certain gator was up to the challenge.

She didn't get to talk to Wes until after the boys were tucked into a motel bed, exhausted by their ordeal. She slipped through the connecting door, shutting it softly, to find a freshly showered Wes watching the television. His face was grim.

"How bad is it?" she asked.

"Take a look." He gestured to the screen, and she

couldn't help but wince at the footage being shown. Animals tearing into each other. Men shooting beasts. Men shifting into animals. Then back. She could only watch in stunned silence.

Even over the stutter of the helicopter blades, she could hear the sounds of screaming, guns firing, and animals snarling. It sounded like a full-on war. And, in a sense, it was. A war to free themselves from the tyranny of a few who thought they should change the status quo. But what would the humans see? Think?

They will see us as monsters. Shiver.

As if sensing her turmoil, Wes wrapped an arm around her and hugged her close. "No shoving it back into a closet now. For better or worse, shifters have been outed."

"Are we okay for tonight?"

"More than okay. I've yet to hear anyone make the connection to Bitten Point yet. Some of those who didn't budge from town say no one's come around. Whatever things Parker and Andrew did to set up the company didn't leave a trail, and your brother and the others made sure to obscure license plates before the invasion."

"Does this mean we can go back home?"

"Maybe. I'll know more in the morning. We can decide then."

She ran a finger down his chest. "We?"

He caught her finger and held it. "Angel, I—"

Stupid man thought he was going to talk, and not to say the right things, judging by the serious look on his face. She wasn't about to let him ruin what they had, not this time.

She put her finger against his lips. "Shh." She replaced that finger with her lips, brushing them against his.

He held himself stiff at first, but she knew his weak points. *I am his weak point.*

She murmured, "Kiss me. Make love to me. Touch me, Wes. I want to feel alive."

What man could resist that plea? Wes didn't even try. With a groan of surrender, he tumbled them back on the bed, his lips taking aggressive control of her mouth. Commanding her lips to open. Dueling with her tongue for dominance.

How she loved this side of him. All man. *All mine.*

It was past time she showed him he wasn't the only one with a need to taste things. She pushed him onto his back and straddled him.

His big hands spanned her waist, and his heavy-lidded eyes perused her. "You are so beautiful," he murmured.

"And you're obviously still under the influence of drugs. My hair is a mess, I'm wearing a man's T-shirt, and I haven't managed to shave any important bits in days."

His lips quirked. "And yet, you've never looked sexier."

He drew her down for a kiss, a slow, sensual teasing embrace that had her fingers digging into his chest and her sex heating. She squirmed atop him, feeling the hard ridge of his erection beneath the fabric of his pants.

Pushing away from him, she sat up and gripped the hem of her shirt. She yanked it over her head, baring herself to his view, wondering if he would care that her breasts hung a little heavier and that her curves were a little more pronounced.

"Fuck me, angel," he breathed, the reverence in his tone clear, but even more telling, in the thickening and pulsing of the cock underneath her.

He likes what he sees.

Nothing like a man's admiration to make a woman want to preen and purr. She arched her back. "Wanna taste?"

With one arm anchored around her waist, he sat up while, at the same time, leaning her back to give him the right angle to tug a nipple into his mouth.

Sweet heaven. The molten tug of his mouth against her nub made her pussy clench. It felt so damned good. He sucked her nipple into his mouth, swirling his tongue around it.

She might have whimpered when he let go, but then she moaned as he grasped the other nipple with his lips and gave it the same torturous attention.

Yes!

He spent a few minutes playing with her breasts, teasing them in turn until she panted and squirmed atop him.

But he wasn't the only one who wanted to play.

She shoved him back down and ordered him to, "Lace your hands behind your head." Her turn to lick something.

Getting to her knees, she crawled backwards, letting her lips tease the taut flesh of his chest, moving lower and lower until she reached the waistband of his pants. Her teeth grabbed the material and tugged. Tugged and got caught on his erect cock.

Grrr. Yeah, she growled with impatience as her fingers had to tug the fabric over his erect shaft. Freed, his dick bobbed upright, long, thick, and oh so yummy looking.

She gripped it, and he hissed. She shot him a warning stare. "Don't move those hands."

He growled back.

Her laughter vibrated his cock as she took him into her mouth. Mmm. The salty drop at the top flavored the big bite. How she loved the feel of him in her mouth. She worked her lips up and down the length of him, tasting every inch, loving how he pulsed at her sucking. How his breathing came harshly at her bobs up and down.

But as much as she wanted to taste all of him, she needed him inside her tonight. Needed that close connection she felt with Wes every time their bodies joined so intimately.

It took only a little maneuvering to position her over his cock. She lowered herself slowly onto it, head thrown back as she took him deep, deeper, until all of him was buried.

Slowly, she rotated her hips, grinding herself on him, pushing until the tip of him hit that sweet spot inside.

He helped her find that rhythm, his hands on her hips, the firm feel of them on her skin so nice. Together they rocked, her pleasure coiling tighter and tighter until, with a scream she had to muffle, with a bite to her lip, she came. The pleasure rolled through her, leaving her limp, so limp she collapsed on his chest.

But Wes held back. He didn't come. He rolled them until she was under him, flat on her stomach. He yanked her ass into the air, exposing her to his view. She clutched at the comforter as he entered her slowly from behind.

Inch. Another inch. A slow, torturous invasion. She could have screamed as her still pulsing flesh stretched to accommodate him once again. Only once he was fully seated did he stop being so damned gentle.

Withdraw. Slam. Over and over he thrust into her welcoming flesh, teasing the remnants of her orgasm and then bringing it to a peak again when he reached under and rubbed her clit as he thrust.

She buried her face in a pillow as he fucked her into a second orgasm, a stronger one that had her yelling into the fabric then almost whimpering as the pleasure proved to be almost too much.

Just when she thought she might die of a never-ending orgasm, which kept her sex quivering and pulsing, he came.

Came with her name on his lips. "Melanie." Came with a growled, "Mine."

Came and then collapsed on her, just like a man. Her man, a man she wrapped her limbs around for a cuddle. A short cuddle before the mommy gene kicked in.

"Put some clothes on."

"What?" he muttered.

"Pants at least," she admonished as she rolled off the bed. She yanked on her T-shirt and located her missing panties. When had those come off? And how had they ended up on the lamp?

She padded away from the bed to open the

connecting door a few inches and peek in. Still sound asleep. Good. She left the door ajar as she returned to Wes sitting on the side of the bed wearing track pants and a bemused expression.

"Get back under those covers and scooch over," she ordered.

"What now?"

She smiled. "Cuddle time."

And sleep, because the events of the day finally caught up, and in the arms of the man she loved, she found peace.

Chapter 24

WAKE UP, dumbass. Someone's in the room.

He fought to keep his eyes closed, even though every nerve tingled as he heard the soft pad of feet, the shushed giggle, smelled the sweet scent of innocence. It was the boys. But why were they up? It was the middle of the night.

Before he could ask them why they were awake, he had to hold his breath and hope that the little hands and knees clambering over his body missed the important bits. It proved close, but his jewels survived a pair of warm bodies worming their way in between him and Melanie. The twins snuggled in, and a few minutes later, the soft whoosh of their breaths let him know they slept. Slept with absolute trust beside him.

The very concept froze him in shock. What did one do when a bed was invaded by little people?

Not just any people.

These are my sons.

His sons.

At least this time he didn't faint at the realization, but it did make him anxious. It also reminded him how woefully inadequate he proved as a father. He'd not only not been there for these kids—and, no, he didn't give himself a free pass on the subterfuge over their creation; he should have known—but add to that the fact he'd played a part in their capture, in Melanie's capture, and in all the shit that happened with Bittech—he was the last person they should be trusting to sleep with.

I've brought them nothing but trouble. And he would continue to do so because it was the Mercer way.

All the self-flagellation came back in an instant, despite Melanie's sweet words and sweeter caresses.

He didn't deserve the woman in this bed, and he most certainly didn't deserve these awesome little boys.

What should he do? What could he do?

I need a smoke.

Easing from the bed, he tugged on a shirt and, from the table by the door, grabbed the pack of cigarettes he'd scored. He headed outside, moving away from the motel itself into the darker shadows at the outer edges of the parking lot.

Boris had driven them for a few hours until he deemed them far enough to stop for the night, and as the grizzled moose stated, "Regroup and plan our next move in the morning." A move that would probably involve them all finding new identities and homes until they could know for sure what their exposure meant.

The question was, what should he do? The last time

Wes had done the right thing, he'd hurt the one person he loved most in the world.

Flick. The tiny flame lit the darkness with orange before setting the tip of his cigarette on fire. The first drag of smoke abraded his lungs, and he coughed. And coughed. The stench of the nicotine repulsed him.

"Filthy goddamned thing." He tossed the offensive butt to the ground. But that wasn't enough. He threw the full pack after it and stomped it. Ground it into the fucking dirt.

"About time you quit."

His head jerked at the sound of his brother's voice. "Brandon?"

Screw his tattered mancard. Wes threw his arms around his brother and hugged him. Hugged him so fucking tight he might have cracked a rib or two.

"I take it you're glad to see me," his brother rumbled.

Releasing him, Wes took a moment to spit on the ground—damned ashtray taste in his mouth lingered—and nonchalantly admit, "Maybe a little."

Brandon laughed. "I'm glad to see you, too, big brother. Although, you weren't easy to follow."

"You followed us?"

"In the sky." His brother looked upward. "Which took some fancy flying considering those freaking helicopters toss around a lot of wind."

Wes reached out and tapped the collar around his brother's neck. "I thought this thing stopped you from going over the fence."

"Those folks that attacked the perimeter knocked the zapping mechanism offline."

"And they freed you."

Brandon shook his head. "I don't know who freed me or the others. I woke up in a cage to see other prisoners running for a secret exit. Turns out there was one hidden at the opposite end."

"What about Sue-Ellen? Did you manage to help her escape before they grabbed you?" *Please let her not have been in the building when it blew.*

"I don't know what happened to her." Brandon shook his head. "Like you, the fuckers darted me before I had a chance to get off the roof. Then, later, when I got out of the below-ground levels, I emerged into a warzone. Guns. And fighting. I took to the air to see what was going on, and that's when I spotted you getting into that. Then everything blew to hell. I figured it was best to follow you. Do you think Susu died in the blast?"

Fuck, he hoped not. It burned Wes to know he'd left without trying to find his sister. Then again, what choice did he have? If captured or detained, he'd do nobody any good. It didn't help the guilt.

"I should have stayed behind and looked for her."

Brandon shoved Wes hard enough he reeled into a tree.

"What the fuck was that for?" he snapped.

"Get off your fucking martyr trip. This isn't your fault. Sue-Ellen. Me. We're not your responsibility."

"You're my family," Wes uttered through gritted teeth.

"Yeah, we are, but that doesn't mean you have to give up everything for us."

Yet, didn't they understand he would? He loved

them, goddammit. Stupid pollen in the air made his eyes water, and he ducked his head.

The rustle of wings made him look up sharply. "Where are you going?"

A sad smile curved his brother's lips as he hovered a few feet above ground. "Somewhere you won't be in danger."

"What are you talking about? We should stick together."

"In that you're wrong. The world knows monsters now exist. Humans know our secret. How safe do you think you'll be if you stick with me?" Brandon gestured to his body. "This is who I am now. I can't hide among the masses like you can. Therefore it's best I leave."

A part of Wes understood why Brandon did it, but it didn't mean he liked it.

Funny because weren't you thinking about doing the same thing? Leaving the people you care about because you think they're better off without you?

"How will I know if you're okay?" Wes asked.

"I'll use that trick Uncle Sammy did when he was smuggling contraband. I'll post ads in the classifieds. Single lizard male is looking to reassure his pussy of a brother he's fine."

Wes couldn't help but snort. "You're an asshole."

"Love you, too, big bro. Stay cool."

With a final salute of farewell, his brother ascended, big wings flapping, another shadow in the sky that Wes soon lost from sight.

Another person he couldn't help. But, then again, his little brother seemed bound and determined to make it on his own. It wouldn't be easy, just like life going forward wouldn't be easy for any of shifter kind. The secret was out. The thing they'd all grown up fearing had come to pass. Such a defining fucking moment in every shifter's life.

But not as defining as knowing Melanie's boys were his.

I'm a fucking father. And it scared the piss out of him.

What did he know of being a dad? What could he offer those kids? Wouldn't it be crueler to taint them with the Mercer name?

Melanie was single again. She could remarry, to a nice guy this time who would—

Oh, like fuck.

Who was he kidding? *I left her once. It almost killed me. I am not leaving her, or my sons, again.*

And anyone who dared to stand in his way would get a big ol' gator welcome.

Snap.

Chapter 25

STANDING AT THE MOTEL WINDOW, Melanie hugged the phone to her ear. "Why are you sighing again?" her mother asked.

Why not? Waking to find the boys in bed and Wes gone left her feeling empty.

He's gone. The thing she'd feared most when she let Wes back into her heart.

Melanie knew her mother wouldn't be sleeping, not with everything that happened, and so she called her, even though she could have just walked a few doors down. While some people might have stayed behind, Daryl ensured their mother hadn't.

"Can't a girl just sigh?" she finally replied to her mother's query.

"No!" her mother retorted.

"I think I'm entitled. I mean, my whole life just got dumped on its ass, and now I've got to figure out a few things."

"Like?"

"Like what to do now that Parker has outed us to the world? Do I take a chance and return to Bitten Point? Go somewhere else? If I do stay, what happens to the house now that Andrew is gone? I mean, according to him, we were no longer legally married, so who gets it now that he's dead?" Did she even want anything associated with that madman?

"Your Uncle Rodriguez will make arrangements. Don't worry about that," her mother declared. Her uncle had a knack for fixing the books. "Why don't you really say what you mean, which is, what should you do about the fact Wes is the boys' father?"

Ah yes, the shocking revelation by Andrew just before he did the world a favor and died. "What of it? I know what he's going to do." She could see it in his eyes. *He's left me again.*

"So don't let him. Your Wes, much like Caleb, has got this stubborn idea in his head that you're better off without him. Isn't that why he dumped you in the first place?" Her mother didn't mince words.

"He dumped me because he was a jerk." Who thought he wasn't good enough for her. Funny, because she'd always thought he was too good to be true.

Did he still believe she deserved better? Dammit, she did. She deserved better than the raw deal she got with Andrew. She deserved something from the guy who donated sperm to make her awesome twin terrors.

She deserved something from the man who made her feel alive again and then ran away the moment he could.

Like hell.

She let him run once, and look what happened.

Chase him down.

Yeah.

Pin him.

Yeah.

Pee on him to mark him as ours.

Um, she was thinking more of a love bite, but yeah!

Time to go stalk my man.

She flung open the motel room door, ready to hunt Wes down if he hadn't gone too far, only to stop dead.

Wes stood in front of the motel door, surprise etched on his face. "Where do you think you're going?"

She arched a brow. "I was coming to get you before you ran away again."

Wes opened his mouth, but before he could speak, she held up a hand. "Don't you dare say a word. I let you do all the talking years ago when you decided what was best for our relationship. And look what happened."

"You married a psychopath who used you in medical experiments."

"I did. And it's all your fault."

A smile tugged his lips at the accusation. "I guess it is. So what are you suggesting I do?"

"First off, you should beg forgiveness for being an ass."

He dropped to his knees, a supplicant before her. "Angel, losing you was the stupidest thing I've ever done."

Her turn to gape.

He winked. "And I'm still a dumb ol' gator, but if

there's one thing I'm smart about it's knowing you are the best damned thing that ever happened to me. I know I've got lots of apologizing to do. And things won't be easy, not with what's happened and all. But I intend to stick by you, no matter what. I want a chance to love you. To protect you. You and our sons. I want to try and be the man you thought I could be."

"Oh, Wes." Tears brimmed in her eyes, and her throat felt tight. "You always were the man I wanted. The one I love." She threw herself into his arms, wrapping him tight. "Don't ever leave me again."

"Never," he said in a fervent promise.

But he froze when a little voice said, "Are you my daddy?"

This time, Wes didn't collapse on his face. He didn't even blanch. He stepped away from Melanie and turned to face the little boys standing side by side in the doorway. Their solemn gazes took in the man who provided half the genes in their body.

Wes sank to his knees. He held open his arms wide. "I am your daddy. And I swear no one"—his voice lowered—"no one will ever harm you or your mother again."

It took the boys only a half second to react. Her twin terrors threw themselves at Wes, and he didn't recoil or push them away. He gathered them in a hug to beat even that of their snake friend, Constantine. Wes held his sons, and dammit, she couldn't help but sob—tears of joy—as she noted the moisture in his eyes.

For better or worse, no matter what the future

brought, they would face the challenge together. As a family. A Mercer family who would show the world what they were truly capable of.

Snap and rawr. Forever.

Epilogue

THE SHIFTER HIGH COUNCIL appointed a spokesperson to deal with the news of their existence. One guess on who was chosen for that role.

The bastard who purposely maneuvered them into revealing their secret took the stage with a great big smile. He wasn't alone. The where-is-Sue-Ellen question got answered. With eyes downcast and hands clasped in front of her was his little sister, still in the clutches of their mad uncle.

But the fact that she lived wasn't the most shocking thing about the news conference. Parker's words were played and replayed on all the news channels. People recited them on the street. Everyone was talking about the revelation.

"My name is Theodore Parker, and I am here to tell you that, yes, shapeshifters do live among you. But despite what you might have seen, or think, you needn't fear. We're just like everybody else."

What a crock of shit.

"Our kind is, with a few exceptions that my company was trying to help, peaceful."

Whopper of a lie.

"We"—Parker drew Sue-Ellen close with a benevolent smile—"look forward to letting you learn about us." Ha. The only thing Parker was interested in learning was what it would take to control those making the laws.

As one of his inner cadre, Brandon knew what Parker was really after. He'd made his intentions quite clear. Being the hidden leader of the SHC wasn't good enough for him. He wanted more power. Wanted a spot in the limelight. So he shoved all of his kind out of the fucking closet into the public eye.

Madman! Despite Parker's announcement, on a live broadcast no less, with a trusted television news anchor, people couldn't forget the other videos. The ones showing their more feral side. Those clips of the battle at Bittech brought a tidal wave of problems.

Humanity felt threatened. Humans felt deceived.

The different became hunted. Laws scrambled to accommodate this unexpected development. Accusation began. Innocents died as neighbor turned on neighbor.

All of Brandon's kind, family and friends, they had to move underground, fight extra hard to appear normal. To appear *human*.

Not everyone could fake it. Brandon certainly couldn't, not with what Bittech did to him.

The world changed, yet Brandon truly didn't care what happened next. The fact that he lived, unchained and able to roam the world, didn't help him.

It didn't make him normal again. When people saw him, they saw the monster.

They screamed.

He got annoyed.

Eat them.

Too often he told his inner self—a now much colder, more cynical dark self—to calm the fuck down. No eating humans.

But they did tempt him, especially when they smelled of chocolate. He still had a sweet tooth.

As he crouched on a rooftop, a living gargoyle observing this new city, yet another place he couldn't blend in, he wondered why he even bothered to try.

Perhaps he should give up on finding answers or help for his monstrous dilemma. He should forget trying to regain normalcy and accept that this new look would stay with him forever. If he melted into the wilderness and lived off the land, maybe he could stop the yearning. Perhaps, in time, he'd forget what it meant to be a man.

A whisper of sound from behind him alerted him he shared the rooftop. He whirled and couldn't help but stare.

Willowy shaped, with long hair the color of moonlight and eyes even stranger than his own, a woman stood. She canted her head to the side, perusing him.

Of most interest, she didn't run. She didn't scream. Inhaling deeply, she tilted her head back, revealing the smooth column of her throat.

Kill her now before she calls for help.

No. He wouldn't kill her, even if all his senses

screamed she meant danger. Dangerous how? All he could see was her fragile beauty—

The impact slammed him to the ground. The air oomphed out of him as her lithe figure landed atop him with more force and weight than expected. A hand, a strong hand tipped in opalescent claws, dug into his throat. Her eyes stared down at him, the orbs slitted and burning with green fire. Her almost pure-white hair lifted and danced around her head.

"What's this roaming my city? A male, both unmarked and unclaimed," she whispered, dipping down low. "I should take you right now."

Perhaps she should. A certain part of him certainly thought so, and it didn't help she squirmed atop him.

The fingers around his throat squeezed, yet no panic infused him. If he was meant to die, then so be it. He tired of hiding.

Her lips hovered devastatingly close, the heat of her breath warming his skin. "How did you come here? Tell me your name."

A name? The one he started the world with no longer seemed to fit. He was more than just a simple Brandon and, at the same time, less than the naïve man he used to be.

"My name is..." Ace? No, he wouldn't use Ace either. That was Andrew's rude misnomer. So what did that leave?

"I am no one, and I come from..." *Don't spread your taint to a town already devastated.* "Nowhere. Who are you? What are you?" Because she smelled like him, but...different.

"What do you mean, what am I?" Her brow crinkled. "I am the same thing you are." Her shoulders drew back, her head tilted imperially, and for a moment, shadowy wings glistened silver at her back. "We are dragon."

TO FIND OUT WHAT HAPPENS WITH *ACE/BRAN- DON,* CHECK OUT *DRAGON POINT.*

THE END

Made in the USA
San Bernardino, CA
16 January 2018